SYDNEY RENEÉ

Let's Be Friends...Always

First published by The Diary of She 2023

First edition

ISBN: 979-8-9878427-0-6

This book was professionally typeset on Reedsy.
Find out more at reedsy.com

I want to dedicate this book to me. Being an author has always been a dream of mine and though it's been a difficult journey it has been a satisfying one. Anything is possible as long as I have my mind, a keyboard, and some faith.

Contents

Acknowledgement

Writing books wasn't my first dream, but it has become my reality. When I decided I wanted to become an author I reached out to the one person who inspired me, Sasha Ravae. Sasha, you have been in my corner since the day I reached out to ask if you were interested in publishing a poetry book. I thank you for having faith in my work. Without you, I wouldn't have published my poetry or gone on to finish that urban fiction I spent 10 years writing.

To my family for always encouraging me and supporting me, but especially to my dad. Dad, I consider you my number one fan and I brag about how much you love my books and push me to submit my work to production companies. One day I'm going to make it happen and the world will see my stories on their TV screens.

A big thanks to my friend Deion Higginbotham, who's a great screenwriter and actor. This series would have never seen the light of day if it weren't for you. I remember sitting at my work desk with nothing to do and talking to you about my short story called *Let's Be Friends*. You read it and your words motivated me to keep writing. I'm grateful to have a creative friend such as yourself.

Finally, I want to acknowledge all of those who have taken a chance on me as an author, whether you enjoyed my stories or not. To those who kept saying, "I can't wait for the next book," when I legit had no plans for there to be another. *Let's Be Friends...Always* wasn't even a thought in my mind, but here we are thanks to you all. I hope you enjoy it!

1

Brandon & Rebecca

"Hurry up! Everyone is waiting and I will not be the one to blame for you showing up late to this very expensive wedding."

"Give us a second little miss missy."

"Mrs. Bloom, I am a grown a..."

"You bet not say it!"

"We'll be right out Mo," Rebecca yelled from the other side of the door before her mother decided to snatch Monica up by the hair and put a beating on her. Monica knew better than to use foul language around her mama.

Rebecca woke up still in disbelief. She had been planning her wedding day for over a year, yet it was still unbelievable. God had blessed her with Brandon Young; a fine, creative, man of God. His unconditional love for her was a bonus. Rebecca hadn't experienced a love like this ever, but she didn't realize it until Brandon opened her eyes. He was truly a dream come true.

Everything she ever wanted had manifested itself; the destination wedding, the man she envisioned spending the rest of her life with, and the people she loved more than anything there to share the special day with her. Shortly the world would officially be calling her Mrs. Young and she couldn't wait.

"How are you feeling baby girl? I know we've been down this road before and unfortunately it was traumatizing for you and all involved."

Athena witnessed first-hand the disaster that was supposed to be her daughter's one and only wedding. The events of that day showed all over Rebecca's face. It was clear she had suffered a great loss and the damage from that relationship took a toll on her for years. How could a man be so cold? To sleep with another woman moments before saying, "I do." Her mother refused to imagine the hell that marriage would have brought. Rebecca didn't believe in divorce. She would have stuck out the marriage in hopes of him becoming a changed man.

"I'm nervous, but I'm extremely grateful to be marrying a man like Brandon. I thought the day would never come, but God answered my prayers. I feel like I'm walking on air just thinking about it. The only thing I'd change is being able to bring daddy back down to earth for this milestone of mine. I know he would have loved to walk me down the aisle. That would have made this day absolutely perfect."

"Another one of your prayers have been answered." Walking over to her purse, Athena pulled out a little emerald box and handed it to Rebecca. When she opened it her eyes landed on a stunning diamond bracelet. Taking the bracelet out the box, Athena lifted Rebecca's right hand and placed the bracelet on her wrist.

"Aww, you didn't have to buy me anything mom."

"This diamond is special," she said pointing to the biggest one in the center, "your father's ashes are in it. I had it made,

2

especially for you."

Rebecca had no words. Embracing her mother in a hug was all she had to offer. Rebecca forced back her tears as she took another look at the bracelet.

"Now he'll be walking the both of us down the aisle," Athena said, kissing her daughter on the cheek.

"Let's get out there before your guest think you ran off."

As Athena and Rebecca made their way towards the door there was Monica with her fist up, ready to knock again.

"About time," she said handing Rebecca her wedding bouquet.

"By the way...love the new bracelet," Monica said before running off.

"Please don't fall," Rebecca screamed after her.

"I'm guessing that girl is still as clumsy as the day I met her."

"She's getting better." Rebecca laughed before closing the door behind her.

* * *

"Damn we look good," Gary said admiring himself in the mirror. "I damn near need to be walking down that aisle too."

"Just like a nigga, trying to make somebody else day about them."

"Well, I mean...why not?" Gary laughed.

"You ain't got no sense," Brandon said fixing his cuffs.

"Only when I'm around my lady. You know she be over my shit."

"Nigga, we all be over your shit."

"Yeah, but I ain't fucking none of y'all so do I really give a fuck? Let me answer that for you. No, No the fuck I don't. On a serious note, I'm proud of you. I always knew out of the two of us, you were going to be the first to put a ring on somebody's finger. I never expected it to be Rebecca, but I wouldn't want to call anyone else my sister. She's as real as they come and the two of you are a match made in heaven. Mom would have absolutely loved her."

"I appreciate it brother. I know mom and pops are here in spirit. They'd be proud of us both. I might be the one getting married, but you've come a long way these last two years."

"Are you niggas crying?" Monica asked, storming into the room.

"Ain't nobody over here crying," Gary spat.

"Yeah, yeah, yeah." Monica giggled. "Brandon it's time for you and Gary to get your asses out there. She's ready!"

"You ready bro?" Gary looked over at Brandon.

"I've never been more ready for anything in my entire life."

"Then let's roll."

2

Here Comes Rebecca

The few that could afford to make it to St Lucia, sat patiently as they waited for the bride to make her appearance. The view the Jade Mountain Resort provided was magnificent and made the wait tolerable despite the heat. Brandon and Rebecca also had the only wedding booked for the day—resort rules, so time was on their side.

There were no more than ten guests and two of them were a part of the wedding party. It was exactly how Rebecca wanted it. She didn't have many friends to begin with and since Brandon was on the outs with Nasir, he only invited one other person besides Gary, who of course was his best man.

When Rebecca decided on a destination wedding Jade Mountain immediately pulled her in. The scenery, seclusion, and ability to make love in the most peaceful place was an automatic win. The thought of looking anywhere else left her thoughts the minute she looked through photos and Brandon was going to go along with whatever his wife-to-be wanted.

"Fall for You" by Leela James began to play and Brandon felt his eyes swelling with tears as he took in his angel. Rebecca stood at the end of the terrace with her mom holding her hand tightly. Brandon couldn't believe the woman standing there was going to be his forever and always.

Rebecca wore an ivory A-line tulle wedding dress with a high split. The top half was made of sequin lace and plunged in the front while remaining open in the back. The dress was made to perfection. For the first time in who knows how long, she decided to wear her hair down and instead of a veil she opted for a simple bridal hairpiece. She was beyond stunning.

"She's beautiful," Gary said placing his hand on his brother's shoulder.

"I don't think there's a word for how magnificent she is," Brandon responded, never taking his eyes off Rebecca.

Everyone began to stand as Rebecca made her way to her husband-to-be. The amount of love surrounding her was nothing as she experienced before—it was overwhelming, but she put on a big smile and held back her joyful tears. There was no way she was fucking up her makeup before the vow exchange.

Approaching Brandon, she wanted to drop her mother's hand and run right into his arms. She felt she couldn't wait a moment longer. She needed to at least feel his fingers laced with hers.

"He's not going anywhere," Athena whispered into Rebecca's ear, sensing her eagerness. "I was the same way with your father."

After what seemed like an eternity, Athena was finally handing her only daughter over to Brandon. "You better treat her with the utmost respect. Treat every day with her as if it will be the last. If I hear otherwise I'll be flying first class on the first flight out to whoop your ass," she said loud enough for everyone to hear.

6

"I know that's right mama," Monica blurted out.

"I like her," Regina could be heard from her seat.

"Trust me, you have nothing to worry about," he said, hugging her before taking his angel's hand and handing Monica her bouquet.

"You didn't have to do that." Rebecca lit up.

"But I did."

"Now that our beautiful bride has arrived, I think it's time that we get this wedding started. But before I do...Is there anyone who dares to hate on this lovely matrimony? If so, I suggest you exit the room because we not having none of that," said Rebecca's best friend Clyde.

After years of not speaking and here he was officiating her wedding. All it took was an invite to a surprise party Brandon had thrown for Rebecca for them to get back on good terms. To her surprise, Brandon had gotten close to Clyde and had been planning the reconciliation for months.

"Oh, get on with it child," Athena said flipping her hand at Clyde.

"Sorry Mrs. Bloom," he said before proceeding.

"Welcome Family and Friends. Today we are here to celebrate Rebecca Bloom and Brandon Young as they become one, legally and spiritually. I have had the honor of knowing Rebecca since we were children and she's the kindest person you will ever meet. Thanks to this brother here, someone so undeserving as myself gets to call her a friend again."

"Yeah, you really lucky 'cause if it weren't for this man here it would have been a wrap," Rebecca chimed in.

"Don't I know it." he smiled at Rebecca before continuing. "As I was saying, it's an honor to bring these two compassion-ate, driven, motivated, and zealous people together. I know this

7

love will be everlasting. With that said, Rebecca and Brandon have chosen to recite their own vows."

Holding Rebecca's hands, Brandon began his vows. He memorized every last word. "My sweet Rebecca, you opened my eyes and my heart to genuine love. The moment we met, God knew you were the one I'd been searching for so desperately. Though you were nothing more than a friend back then, time spent with you has always been heaven-sent. From random trips to bookstores and coffee spots, I knew nothing about it. Everything we did I stored away in my heart and vowed to never forget. Since then, my heart only grows bigger making way for more memories with you."

Noticing the tears beginning to flow down his cheek, Rebecca slipped her hand away and softly removed them from his face. Brandon took that same hand, kissing it before continuing. "I vow to be there for you until I'm no longer on this Earth. Not only when times are good, but those moments you are at your lowest. I promise to forever watch over you, even in death. I promise to always communicate my feelings, and to be honest even when it's hard because your trust in me I never want to lose. I promise to always support you, not only financially, but in your career and everything in between. I look forward to learning more about you and falling deeper in love with you with each day that passes. Thank you for being my best friend and now my wife. I love you eternally."

By the end of his vows, everyone was in tears, including Rebecca.

"That was beautiful," Clyde said. "Are you ready to share your vows, Rebecca?"

"Here you go," Monica said passing Rebecca a handkerchief. She gently patted her face to avoid ruining her makeup any more than she may have already.

"I do not know how I'm going to top that, but let me try." She sniffled. "I had some words written down, but I think I'm going to speak from the heart."

"Brandon, my rainbow through the storm. When times got hard you stood by my side without me having to ask. You were the last person I expected to come around and offer me a shoulder to cry on. You were there to stop me from doing things I knew I would regret. Honestly, you were the last person I expected to fall madly in love with. I was hesitant, but you are the one person and one choice I will never regret. To think I almost missed out on a husband because of my morals. For as long as I live I am committed to loving you, uplifting you, trusting you, and learning you inside and out. I thank God for sending you my way. You weren't only what I wanted but what I needed and will continue to need. You understand me when I don't even understand myself. I'm blessed...blessed to have you. You make me a better person, a confident person. With you, everything is clear. Brandon, you never, and when I say never, I mean never have to question this love. I'm riding until we can't ride anymore. When we no longer exist in this lifetime, I know our love will exist in the next and the next one after that. It's me and you for an eternity. I love you!"

Everyone stood up and applauded as if they had just watched the greatest performance of a lifetime.

"And with these words, I now pronounce you husband and wife," Clyde announced.

Brandon and Rebecca kissed each other as if they were the only two left on the entire island.

3

Introducing Mr. & Mrs. Young

"How does it feel to be a married woman?"

"It hasn't hit me yet, but what I do know is I'm ready to see what that husband dick is hitting for," Rebecca said, raising her hands to the heavens.

"I swear you get nastier by the second," Nikki said proudly. "I remember when you could barely say the word dick."

"Well, that's what happens when one of your closest friends writes books about people fucking for a living. I've pocketed a few of those skills you wrote about," Rebecca admitted.

"Mrs. Young...I would love to say fuck all these people and have you show me a few of those skills right now," Brandon said sneaking up behind Rebecca.

"I want you to keep that same energy for the rest of this trip cause I ain't letting up. I don't want to hear none of that oh baby I'm tired give me a few hours' bullshit."

"You two better calm down before your mama come over here and whoop everybody's ass," Monica said, sneaking behind Nikki. Monica placed her arms around her waist and then planted a kiss on the neck.

"You really are scared of her, aren't you honey?" Nikki laughed.

"If you spent time at Rebecca's house you would be too. She was no joke."

"Well, if you ask me, she's focused on trying to get some action for herself tonight." Brandon pointed towards the bar. Athena was standing there flirting with the bartender. Rebecca couldn't understand what was so funny. She might have been a widow, but she was not about to be getting her groove back with some youngin' working their reception.

"Uh uh, she needs to calm it down. Someone tell Gary to get her."

"Shit, I don't know she might start flirting with him too," Brandon joked.

"I wouldn't even be mad, my man is fine," Regina chimed in.

"You do know your man is identical to my husband," Rebecca jokingly said, side-eyeing Regina.

"Nah, your husband is rougher around the edges."

"Get the fuck out of here," Brandon said throwing his hands in the air. "Everyone here knows that I'm the smooth one."

Breaking up the bickering about who is the better-looking twin, Kim said, "Don't worry. Me and Nick will go sit with her."

"Thank you, Kim," Rebecca said hugging her.

"Excuse me, Mrs. Young," the photographer interrupted, "can I borrow you two for a while? We'd like to get some pictures of you and the Mr. and after we can get some of you guys with your guest."

"We'll be right there."

A few minutes later, Rebecca and Brandon walked hand-in-hand to the terrace pathway while the guest remained on the rooftop for cocktails. The views were astonishing, and

Rebecca couldn't wait to show off their pictures. The walls in the new house would be covered in them. Jade Mountain was truly a magical place and Rebecca was in pure bliss. They were surrounded by the sea, greenery, blue skies, and jagged mountains.

Once the photographer captured pictures on the Celestial Terrace, they made their way back to the rooftop to get some pictures with the group before heading to the sanctuary to get photos in the infinity pool.

* * *

Brandon and Rebecca sat at the head of the table, backs facing the sea. On Rebecca's side sat her mother, Monica, Regina, and Kim. On Brandon's side sat Clyde, Nikki, Gary, and Nick. Lining the center of the table were a ton of white and brown roses and candles in glass holders. Soft music played as they enjoyed some of the Bride and Grooms' favorite meals. Starting with a shrimp cocktail, mini crab cakes, and a small Caesar salad. For their entrees, they were served filet mignon, grilled shrimp, roasted potatoes, and creamed spinach.

"What a delicious meal princess, you guys did well."

"Thank you, mom, but it was mostly Brandon."

"Your daughter was going to have all of you drunk and starving. The only thing she wanted to serve y'all were a few appetizers...and I mean very few."

"Hmm, I wonder why?" Monica snickered.

"She's trying to make sure she doesn't come busting out that dress," Kim responded. "If it was my wedding day, we'd all be starving. So heads up, when I do get married make sure you show up with your bellies full because y'all won't be eating a thing." She laughed

"Can I propose before you go inviting everyone to our wedding? See what you two started?" Nick said, glaring down at Brandon and Rebecca.

"We're just two people in love," Brandon said, kissing his wife.

"Well, once Rebecca gets to throwing that bouquet we'll see which of you three couples are next," Athena said.

"Glad I don't have to worry about that anytime soon," Clyde expressed.

"Thank goodness 'cause nobody wanted to watch you marry that psychopath."

"I'm with the wifey. The things you disclosed about that chick...Glad you got out safe," Brandon said shaking his head.

"Damn, that bad?" Gary asked.

"You don't even want to know," Brandon and Rebecca said together.

"Enough of that," Monica interjected. Picking up her champagne glass, she stood up and began her speech. "I would like to raise a glass to my best friend in the whole world. I know we've had our ups and downs, but through it all, we've always managed to get our shit back tight. Without our friendship, I probably would have been behind someone's jail by now." Monica chuckled. "I am so proud of the woman you are. You push me to strive for excellence and I'm truly happy you are getting all you deserve. Here's to you and your amazing husband."

Everyone raised their glasses and took a sip.

"Me next!" Nikki jumped up. "When I met Rebecca, I was a new author who hadn't a clue what she was doing. Rebecca was there to guide me every step of the way. She's been a mentor, a friend, and she probably could have been my girlfriend." Nikki winked at Rebecca and they both blushed. "Then the day came that I wanted to take my career a step further. That's when Brandon and my beautiful girlfriend Monica came into the picture. Thanks to you two I now have a group of friends I can call family. I wish the two of you nothing but happiness, love, health, and continued success. Love you, guys!"

"We love you too." Rebecca smiled.

"Alright ladies, give the men a chance to say something. That's if you guys would like," Athena said. "Except you Clyde, you already said enough today."

"Mom." Rebecca shook her head.

Gary stood up with a butter knife and his glass, clinking them together. "To my baby brother...by 5 minutes," Gary chuckled, "I expressed this to you before you exchanged vows with your lovely wife, but I'm going to say it again...I am proud of you and the woman you chose. Not only would mom approve, but the two of them would have been the best of friends. Rebecca, you may have thought I didn't like you, but you've always been an amazing woman to be around and I'm honored to call you my sister. I wish you two nothing but the best and I can't wait to see where life takes this union."

"Thank big bro," Brandon said getting up to hug him.

"I really appreciate that Gary. I'm also happy to be able to call you my brother as well. You might get on my nerves, but I love you. Especially the *you* that Regina was able to tame. Salute to you my love," Rebecca said raising her glass towards Regina.

"It wasn't hard to do." She laughed and then blew a kiss at Gary.

"May I speak?"

"Of course, you can Kim," Brandon said sweetly.

14

4

First Night as Husband & Wife

Brandon and Rebecca couldn't keep their hands off each other as they made their way to the honeymoon suite. By the time they walked through the door, his shirt was unbuttoned and her dress was unzipped. Thank goodness the resort was adults only because if it took a minute longer to get to their room, someone was going to get a free show.

The resort provided the best suite they had to offer newly-weds; located on the highest level of the resort and provided a 24/7 panoramic view of the water and mountains. Rebecca's favorite feature was the infinity pool and she couldn't wait for Brandon to fuck her in it.

"Don't take it off yet," Rebecca demanded when Brandon tried to pull off her dress. "Bend me over and fuck me with it on."

"I want to look deep into your eyes," Brandon said.

"We've got all night," Rebecca said unzipping his pants, sliding her hand inside to stroke his long thick shaft, "but right here, right now...I want you to fuck me like a slut."

Rebecca licked Brandon's lips and turned around to rest her

torso on the sofa in front of them.

"You just don't know how hard you get me when you talk that freaky shit."

"Less talking and more action. I need to feel every inch," she said looking back at him with hunger in her eyes.

Doing as told, Brandon lifted Rebecca's dress and snatched off her thong with ease, sending a quiver through her body. Spitting on his fingers, he glided them across her lower lips using his thumb to massage her clit. Rebecca's pussy throbbed, calling for Brandon's manhood to beat away at her insides. Entering her slowly, the warmth of her almost made him explode causing him to back out.

"Don't run from it Daddy." Rebecca slammed herself back against him. "FUCK ME!"

Gripping her hair, Brandon pounded away at Rebecca's love. She matched his rhythm with every stroke. Looking down at his dick, Rebecca's juices glistened all over it.

"Faster Daddy," she screamed out as she came uncontrollably.

Pulling out, Brandon turn Rebecca over and placed her on the edge of the sofa, ripping her dress at the split. Wrapping his hand around her neck, they looked each other deep in the eyes as their bodies thrust against one another.

"Got damn! you're soaking wet."

"Don't cum yet," Rebecca moaned out, feeling Brandon's dick pulsate inside of her.

Pulling out, Brandon spread her legs and entered her with his fingers. Taking them out, he rubbed her juices around her lips and then placed them in her mouth, admiring her while she sucked them clean.

"Tell me how you taste?"

"Enticing."

"Exactly how I like," he said dropping to his knees to kiss her sweet lips.

Brandon bit at her thighs, knowing the slightest pain drove Rebecca insane. Placing her hand on the back of his head she moved him back to her center, allowing him to take in every drop of nectar. Rebecca never removed her hand as she moved up and down on his face, letting the waves of ecstasy take over. Brandon drank every ounce of her love and then licked up the leftovers.

Rebecca's body was drained yet she still wanted more. Moving from the couch she walked Brandon to the bed, sitting him on the edge. Brandon admired his wife as she let the remainder of her dress drop to the floor. Lowering in front of him, she took hold of his smooth chocolate dick and started teasing it with her tongue, never taking her eyes off Brandon.

"Damn, you're sexy," he groaned.

Opening her mouth she wrapped her lips around the tip, licking and sucking while she used one hand to massage the rest and the other to play with his balls. The more spit that dripped down his shaft the further she took him in. Eventually, Rebecca could feel him in the back of her throat and she was impressed with herself. From the sounds escaping her husband, he was too.

"Baby, I'm about to cum."

Loving the taste of Brandon, she continued to choke on his dick, watching one hand grip the sheets while the other took hold of her hair. With one last slurp, his cum shot into the back of Rebecca's throat. Swallowing every drop, she continued to suck on Brandon's manhood until he couldn't take anymore.

"Fuck," he grunted as his legs began to quiver.

"Delicious," Rebecca said licking her lips.

The sight alone shot Brandon's dick up again.

"I'm pleased to see you're not tapping out," Rebecca said sliding herself onto his erection. "Can you handle another go-round?" Rebecca moved up and down as she talked to Brandon. "I hope you say yes," she said pushing him down on the bed, fucking him slowly.

"Does this answer your question?" He said lifting himself enough to suck on Rebecca's breast.

Rebecca and Brandon made love for hours, eventually falling asleep in each other's arms. Waking up a few hours later, Rebecca spotted Brandon standing on the balcony by the infinity pool, taking in the fresh air. They still had a few hours before the sun rose.

Walking over to him, still naked, she wrapped her arms around his waist. "What are you doing up?"

"My body is telling me I need to enjoy this place. Sleep will come later."

"It is a dream," she said kissing his back.

"Magical," he replied, taking hold of her hand.

"Hey, let's take a shower, then we can stay up and watch the sunrise together," Rebecca suggested.

Once in the shower, they cleaned each other's bodies and Brandon washed Rebecca's hair.

"We need to do this more often."

"Take showers?" Rebecca said sarcastically, laughing at her attempt at making a joke.

"No silly. Share more intimate moments like this. We've been so caught up in both our businesses that we rarely get this much time to just peacefully enjoy one another."

"Whatever you want my love," Rebecca said, turning around

to kiss her husband.

"I want you," he said lifting her against the shower wall.

Rebecca wrapped her legs around him tight, inviting him in. Gripping onto her ass, Brandon welcomed himself, embracing her love with long slow strokes as he kissed her intensely. Never in his life had he needed a woman the way he needed Rebecca. Brandon could feel her walls tightening around his dick as he made love to her once again. The water flowed over them as their bodies continued to collide with one another. Wrapping her arms tightly around his neck, Brandon placed his hands firmly against the wall as Rebecca bounced herself up and down on his chocolate delight. They were both ready to cum...and they did.

"I love you, husband."

"I love you more wife."

5

Brandon & Rebecca Move

Seven days spent in paradise and now it was time to deal with the real world. No more personal spa treatments or sharing breakfast in bed. The outstanding view and seclusion of the beautiful island were no longer within their reach. They were back in the City of Angels where work and boxes of their belongings awaited them.

Rebecca's mom Athena made her way back to Seattle two days after the wedding, promising to come to spend more time with Rebecca in Los Angeles. It wasn't her scene, but being in St. Lucia with her daughter reminded her of how much fun they used to have together. Rebecca in return made a promise to check in more often and to visit at least 4 times throughout the year. Rebecca spent almost all of her twenties building a successful brand and career, causing her to forget who mattered most; her mother. Brandon vocalized the importance of holding on tight to that relationship. On a daily, he longed for his mother. He wished he could spend time with her and call her at any given moment.

Kim and Nick had to go home the next day to get back to her

daughter Ari. Laura and her mother were on babysitting duty, but Kim hated being away for too long. It made her anxious knowing that if anything were to happen she couldn't get to her baby girl immediately. Rebecca loved how dedicated she was to her child. She prayed one day she got the chance to experience a mother's bond with her own child. The rest of the crew stayed for the remainder of the trip, but they rarely crossed paths except for the times they'd gather for dinner or occasionally see each other in passing. The rest of the trip turned into a private baecation for all parties remaining.

Instead of returning to work right away, Rebecca decided to take one more week off to make sure the movers didn't fuck up anything and to get things organized. Brandon was starting production on a new pilot show and she didn't want anything distracting him. The old house was all packed up, and they had received the keys to their new house before heading to St. Lucia.

Brandon and Rebecca decided to move out of busy LA and into the suburbs of Calabasas. The commute to work would suck, but since Diane made Rebecca part owner of **Pretty & Bold** she was able to create her schedule. Brandon would be back and forth a lot, but they agreed it would be best for them to build their family outside of LA. Brandon was going to miss his home, but it was time to move on. That was the first house he bought when he got big and his wife did not need a daily reminder of the bachelor life he lived there. It was time to come new. To Brandon, the new house felt like a downgrade, but Rebecca loved it. To her, it was still huge, but it had a more homely vibe. Brandon still had his pool and theater room. The bonus for him and Rebecca was the gym, library, and separate walk-in closets. There would be no arguing over how much space each of them could use. In all reality, their new home was nothing short of perfect.

"Is that everything Mrs. Young?" One of the movers called out to her.

"Yes, that's everything. I'm going to do one last run-through, but I will meet you at the house. My best friends, Clyde and Monica will be waiting there to help."

"Sounds good. We will see you soon," he said, signaling for the rest of the movers to get going.

"Shall we make love one last time?" Brandon came walking down the stairs.

"I don't know about love, but we can fuck."

"When did you get so vulgar? Does your mother know you speak in this manner?"

"I think she has an idea," Rebecca said, meeting Brandon at the island in the kitchen.

"Well, I think I need to fuck some politeness into you."

"Sounds like a win-win for me."

The honeymoon might have been over, but Brandon and Rebecca were still going at it like dogs in heat. Something about officially being married heightened the passion between them. Whenever an opportunity presented itself they found themselves in all kinds of positions. Lifting Rebecca onto the island, he pulled her shirt over her head revealing her breast. Her nipples were erect, calling out for Brandon's juicy lips. Cupping them with his massive hands, he sucked and kissed them one at a time.

"Yes," Rebecca moaned, tugging at his sweats.

Brandon helped her pull them off and she undid her jeans as they tongued each other down. Once he had her fully undressed he spread her thighs, placing her right leg over his shoulder. As Brandon continued to kiss Rebecca he teased the opening of her sex with the tip of his dick, ensuring she was nice and wet before diving in. Unable to take anymore, Rebecca took hold of his manhood and guided him into her awaiting love.

"Oh my God," she screamed out as Brandon pounded against her. Her moans echoed throughout the house.

"Turn over and poke that ass out for me."

Following his command, Rebecca lay across the island with one leg bent, providing him a full view of her glistening holes. Brandon watched his dick go in and out of her love, each time wetter than before.

"Harder Daddy," she moaned.

Taking hold of her neck, Brandon thrashed into her, getting more aroused by the sound of her ass smacking against his stomach. As Brandon continued to fuck the soul from Rebecca, he slid his thumb into her butt, causing her to squirt all over him, the floor, and slightly on the countertop.

"Fuck," Rebecca whimpered, Brandon still stroking her insides, causing another wave to come over her.

With one last stroke, Brandon let himself go, pulling Rebecca back up against his chest. He held onto her tight until every drop of his cum was floating inside of her.

"Who's going to clean this up?" She laughed.

* * *

"Bout time you guys showed your faces." Monica rolled her eyes at Rebecca. "The movers are practically done."

"Nah for real," Clyde added, "we expected y'all would be about 30 minutes behind but two hours. What the fuck was y'all doing?"

"Do you really want to know?" Rebecca said grinning wide.

"I don't. I'm about to go sit down on that nice comfy couch. You two can take over," Clyde said walking back inside.

"I'm right behind you," Brandon yelled out.

"Really husband?"

"Sorry Wifey, my legs hurt from driving." He winked and then proceeded to kiss Rebecca on the cheek.

"You lucky y'all still newlyweds or I'd be pissed right now." Monica shook her head.

"I'm sorry Mo. It's been impossible to keep my hands off him. I've been so damn horny."

"Well I need you to get your head out of the cloud of dicks it's in and come inside to help me with these boxes. All Clyde's ass did was tell them where to put the furniture. He hasn't moved shit."

"That sounds about right." Rebecca giggled.

"See, this is why I date women. Men ain't worth a damn."

"I don't know about all men, but mine is incredible."

"Incredibly lazy," Monica said looking over at Brandon drinking a beer on the couch alongside Clyde.

"He deserves it." Rebecca blushed.

"You make me sick."

"Don't be jealous." Rebecca teased.

"Nope, I'm jealous. I could have been home in bed with my lady still. I want to have nasty sex too." Monica laughed.

"I'm sure Nikki gives you plenty. Speaking of, how has living together been? I know she was nervous."

"It's been amazing actually. She's extremely nurturing and I wasn't aware I needed that in my life. It's nice to come home to her after a long day of shoots. I will admit she tripped out on me one night though. She's scary as fuck when she's upset."

"You know them Dominican women don't play. Anyways

let's go get the dishes put away so we can share a glass of champagne," Rebecca said walking towards their chef-sized kitchen. "So, I was thinking about having a housewarming in about a week or so and wondered if I should invite Ashley."

"ASHLEY!"

"What about Ashley," Brandon said walking over to the kitchen.

"Thanks a lot, Mo." Rebecca nudged her.

"Maybe we should go," Monica said chugging her champagne and rushing over to Clyde before Rebecca could protest.

"Um, I guess I'll see you guys another day," Clyde shouted as Monica dragged him out the door.

"What is this I hear about Ashley?"

"I was just saying it would be nice to invite her to our housewarming."

"Ashley...Ashley, Ashley?" Brandon said confused.

"Yes, Ashley Ashley. You know she doesn't really have any friends. Regina is always hanging with us, her brother and his girlfriend barely spend time with her."

"That's not our fault," Brandon said walking over to hug Rebecca, "and she has Nicole."

"I know, but I still feel bad. It's not like she'd be bringing Nasir with her. He can stay home with the baby and she can come enjoy herself."

"I'm not sure I like the idea, but you're right. This can give her some time to spend with Nick and Kim."

"Thank you for being an understanding husband," she said kissing him on the lips. "Now let's work on getting this place together before no one gets to come over."

"Can I work on you first?" He asked.

"That'll always be a yes."

6

Monica & Clyde

"So, are you going to tell me why we rushed out of there," Clyde said leaning back in the passenger seat.

"I wouldn't say rushed," she laughed, "but the mention of Ashley was the perfect excuse for us to make our exit."

"What's the deal with her and this Ashley? Didn't she sleep with her ex and now they have a baby together?

"She sure did.

"So how did they suddenly become friends?"

"About a year and a half ago, at Ashley's baby shower, some crazy shit went down during the middle of it. I can't say exactly what because I wasn't invited. But apparently, Rebecca was the only person to go and make sure Ashley was doing okay. Ashley apologized for her part in the breakup with Nasir and from there they formed their little friendship."

"Women are so strange," Clyde uttered.

"Says the guy who breaks off his friendship with his best friend every time he gets in a relationship."

"It's not even like that," Clyde said looking straight ahead.

"Then what is it like? One minute you two are inseparable and the next you turn to Casper, the rude version. I almost forgot you existed," Monica said looking at him and then back towards the road. "You know she needed you around when she was going through her breakup with Nasir. Thank goodness Brandon and Nikki were around because I wasn't the best of friend during that time myself."

"Trust me, every moment without her in my life I felt like shit, but the feelings I had for her at the time were starting to exceed friendship. If you can...imagine how confusing that was for me. I couldn't even tell you the moment I started feeling like we could be something more than friends. I could only imagine how she would have felt if I acted on those feelings, especially while she had a man."

That was a confession Monica was not prepared to hear, but it didn't make sense to her. Clyde seemed to always be in a relationship, so at what point did his feelings for Rebecca begin to grow and how come she never picked up on it? *Maybe they were always there and he just hid them behind other women*, she thought to herself.

"So, you stopped speaking to her because you were falling in love?"

"Yes," Clyde confessed.

"And what about now...How do you feel about her?"

"I'm happy for her and I'm glad she's back in my life. At one point she was the only person I had, but seeing her with Brandon and knowing she's in good hands puts me at ease."

"That wasn't the question Clyde..."

"Do I need to spell it out? No, I'm not in love with Rebecca anymore. It's been about 5 years now and our friendship is what's important to me. I let any possibility of being with her go when she started dating Nasir anyway," he replied. "I promise you don't have to worry about me coming between her marriage or disappearing from her life again. I'm here to stay. Plus, I like being around everyone...I wouldn't jeopardize that."

"Good to know. I am not trying to be wrapped up in any more love triangles. Lord knows this group has had way too many of those."

"Yeah, y'all was swapping bodily fluids like a muthafucka." He busted out in laughter.

"Where the fuck am I dropping you off?"

7

Monica & Nikki

"What took you so long? You've been gone for hours and we had plans."

"I am so sorry kitten," Monica said trying to butter up Nikki before she got upset. "I promise you I didn't mean to take this long, but Brandon and Rebecca are still in the honeymoon phase," Monica said walking over to the couch to sit with Nikki.

Nikki giggled. "Let me guess, instead of meeting you at their new place he was introducing his penis to her vagina again?"

"How'd you know?"

"They're newlyweds. Something about a legalized commitment turns women on and my girl is a freak now. But if we're being real, I think she's working on a baby."

"What do you know that I don't?" Monica asked. Although she was Rebecca's bestie, Nikki always seemed to have the scoop before she did.

"I know she wants a baby and since finding out she can safely carry, why not try?"

When Rebecca shared her concerns with Nikki and Brandon

about possibly being infertile, she decided to set up an appointment. Brandon, along with Rebecca had to undergo several tests, but the doctor found nothing wrong. Rebecca was healthy and the doctor was confident that between her egg count and Brandon's sperm, they'd be able to conceive quickly.

"True, but what's going to happen to the show you two have, and what about the publication?"

"You do know women can work and still take care of children right?" Nikki reminded Monica. "Even if she does have to take a break from the podcast, I've gotten to the point where I can carry the show on my own. There's no need for you to worry. You just keep booking those commercials and films."

"Speaking of...Brandon has a new show he's working on and he asked me to be a part of it, but I'm not sure I want to."

"That's big. What's stopping you?"

"I don't want to be known as the woman who only appears in GB Entertainment productions," Monica answered.

"I understand, but their production quality is getting better especially Brandon's side production company. They were the first to truly take a chance on you."

"It's not about the quality. I want to feel like I'm making it in this industry on my own, not because my friend is married to the man in charge," Monica admitted.

"No one knows his wife is your best friend and he saw your potential way before Rebecca was his wife."

"But I know and it's starting to bother me."

"The best advice I can give you is to keep an open mind. Look over the script and see if the role fits you, but still work on getting booked for other projects outside of Gary and Brandon. You don't have to limit yourself to commercials and short films, but you should keep getting your face out there. Whatever you choose to do I'm here to support you," Nikki said pulling Monica's face closer to hers.

"That's why I love you. You've been my biggest supporter since the beginning," Monica said kissing Nikki.

"Can I say something without you getting offended?" Nikki asked.

"Of course."

"You don't smell so great," she said covering her nose. "I think you should go take a shower and I'll be right here. Take your time."

"Wow babe, you could have said something before I sat my stank ass on the couch."

While waiting for Monica to get freshened up, Nikki pulled out her phone to order food. She was thinking Mexican and then she would make them some margaritas. Once the food was ordered Nikki opened up the windows to let in some fresh air and lit her favorite candles.

"Do you still want to go out to eat," Monica yelled from the bedroom about forty minutes later.

"The food is here," Nikki announced after hearing a knock at the door.

"Great!"

Monica came out of the bedroom with a long T-shirt on and her braids in a bun. There was no point in getting dressed if they were going to lounge around for the night.

"Please tell me they remembered the salsa this time," Monica said walking over to the counter.

"You know I made it very clear they better not forget."

"Should we eat at the table like normal people?" Monica asked,

"Sure, we can make this our date night since Rebecca kept

you busy today."

While Nikki plated their food and arranged it on the table like they were at a restaurant, Monica put on some music and brought a few candles over to the table. Nikki made her way back to the kitchen to make a pitcher of Margarita.

"Look at you being all fancy," Monica said watching her make drinks. "You know you're stunning right?"

"Obviously."

8

Ashley

When Ashley woke up, she noticed a message on her phone from the night before but hadn't looked at it until now. Little Nasir ran her wild all morning and the last thing on her mind was checking messages, but once she did she had to take a triple look to confirm what she was seeing.

> **Rebecca:** *In about a month me and Brandon are having a housewarming and I wanted to invite you. Bring your sister along if you'd like. If you don't mind it'll be an adults-only party; drinking, dancing, and swimming. I'm sure you could use a break, so put Nasir on daddy duty and come let loose lol.*

Rebecca would occasionally check in on Ashley and the baby, especially after the drama that happened at her baby shower. Never in a million years did she think they would have anything close to a friendship. If it were Ashley, she probably would have never forgiven the woman who slept with and got pregnant by her boyfriend, but Rebecca was more mature than most. Every part of Ashley wanted to dislike her, but it was practically impossible. Even her brother had come to love Rebecca and Nick rarely liked anyone. She could barely get him to come around Nasir and it ate her up inside, but she understood the position he was in. Kim still wasn't comfortable coming anywhere near Nasir. She said she had forgiven him, but forgiving someone wasn't the same as forgetting. Seeing Nasir was a constant reminder of the trauma she experienced. It may have only been one night, but the damage was stuck with her for a lifetime. To pretend it didn't happen would have been insane.

Ashley: Lol he can take over for a day. I could use a little break. I will extend the invite to Nicole.

Rebecca: Great! Can't wait to see you. I hope everything is good with you and the baby by the way.

Ashley: We are doing good. He is walking now and running into walls like he's been hyped up on sugar all day.

Rebecca: Aww! I know his first birthday was some months ago. Sorry, we couldn't make it. I hear 1st birthdays are the best. I'll be sure to have a gift for him when you come for the warming. I'll update you with the address and time once I decide on the exact date. Talk to you soon.

"God, I hate how nice she is," Ashley said out loud.

"Who?"

"Why are you always so nosy? Aren't you supposed to be spending time with your nephew?"

"You're the one talking out loud and secondly, how am I supposed to spend time with a sleeping child?" Nicole said, rolling her eyes.

"I'm sorry. That child wore both of us out this morning. What child wakes up at 5 in the morning, faithfully? He just like his damn daddy."

"Yeah, I don't miss any of that, especially Nasir and that loud-ass blender." Nicole shook her head thinking about it.

About six months after moving in with Ashley, Nicole found a one-bedroom apartment about twenty minutes from Ashley and Nasir's. As much as she loved being a room away from her nephew, she could not stand the sexual tension between Ashley and Nasir. They had entirely too much history between each other and Nicole didn't understand how they could live with one another, but not be together. They loved each other, but Ashley knew their relationship wouldn't survive as long as he was still dealing with shit she wanted to be a part of.

"Since you insist on knowing—"

"I don't...but you can continue," Nicole replied.

"Rebecca would like for us to attend her housewarming next month."

"Rebecca, thee Rebecca?"

"Yes, the only Rebecca I know."

"I'm down, but is *he* going to be fine with that."

"Probably not, but that's his problem, not mine. The woman is nice as hell and pretty hard to say no to. I see why he fell for her. Shit, I like her myself," Ashley confessed. "Something about her brings the good out of everyone."

"You might be right. Nick gushes over her relationship with Brandon and how kind she is to his girlfriend. I still can't believe they went to her wedding."

"It was beautiful right?" Ashley added.

"Why are you two in here all excited?" Nasir came walking into the living room.

"Nothing at all," Nicole lied.

"Then why are you guys smiling like that? It's kind of scary. Did I do something wrong?"

"Okay you caught us," Ashley said, "Nicole is thinking about dating again and I'm just excited for her."

"I'm wha—" Nicole almost blurted out before being cut off by Ashley.

"I'm going to help her set up her dating profile."

"Happy to hear you're finally moving on from that asshole," Nasir replied. "Anyways I was coming to let you know I'm running out to show a listing. I should only be gone for two hours max. Are you going to be okay?" Typically Nasir had Sundays off, but if it was an important client he would make room in his schedule.

"I'll be fine. I'm sure Nicole will be here for a while."

"She's right. I miss my munchkin."

"As if you don't see him every other day. I'll call you on the way back to see if you want something to eat." Nasir leaned down and kissed Ashley on the forehead then made his exit.

"Really? A dating app Ashley." Nicole laughed. "Why couldn't you just tell him?"

"So he could freak out? He was already in his feelings about my brother being at his exes' wedding. How do you think he's going to react when I tell him we're going to her house? He's legit being left out of all of Brandon's big moments."

"If you think about it...he's the only one making things weird. Everyone speaks to each other except him, Brandon, and Rebecca. Gary is Junior's godfather for fucks sake and Brandon couldn't even come to his first birthday," Nicole practically shouted.

"I know. I never thought their friendship would crumble the way it has, but until he and Brandon stop holding on to that hurt and deceit this is the way things have to be. I know they miss each other, but you know men and their pride."

"Before this housewarming, you need to figure out a way to tell Nasir before all hell breaks loose. You two seem to be on good terms and I'd hate for one little secret to ruin that," Nicole warned her.

"I promise I'll figure it out."

9

Nasir

Within 45 minutes Nasir had completed showing his listing. His client had previously expressed how he wanted to put down a cash offer immediately, but Nasir wanted him to do one walk-through before making a final decision. Nasir had previously sold the same house to Diane and not even a year later she was putting it back on the market. Shortly after Nicole called off her engagement with Derek, Diane found out about the double life he was leading. Nasir figured it was Rebecca who told her. Feeling guilty, Derek put the house in Diane's name thinking it would keep her from leaving him, instead, she came up on a bag.

Nasir still had time to kill but no one to kill it with. The crew was now split up, so he was only able to see Gary now and then. Nasir's social life included work, his son, and Ashley. On occasion, he would go on outings with the agents at his company, but he didn't like being the boss that hung out with his employees all the time. It wasn't a good look; one because most of his employees were women and two, one had a huge crush on him that Ashley couldn't stand.

I really don't have any friends, Nasir thought as he scrolled through his phone, seeing who he could call. Ultimately, he only had one person he knew would pick up.

"Hey," he greeted Ashley through the phone, "I'm done so I'm going to head back to the house. Did you want me to get you food?"

"No, I'm not hungry."

"What are you guys up to?"

"Just sitting here watching your son run around like a baby crackhead."

He laughed as he imagined his son falling all over the place. "Wow, don't get at my son like that. Record it for me though."

"Already beat you to it. Check your phone."

In his messages were three videos of Little Nasir. Seemed like yesterday when he started walking and now he was running marathons around his mother. When he and Ashley decided to be friends, he was unsure how they'd co-parent. Would he have gotten to see all of his son's small wins, or how his little face and body changed with each day? It was the greatest blessing that came from his fucked decision-making.

"That boy is something else."

"Ain't he?" Ashley giggled.

"You sure you don't want anything before I come back?"

"I'm positive. Go enjoy some time alone," Ashley insisted. "Me and Nicole will be just fine. Go to a movie or take a run. I know you got your gym bag in the backseat."

"I'd much rather be home with you two."

"I know, but you really need to get some friends before you turn into one of those uncool dads." She laughed.

"Wow there, that'll never happen." Nasir pretended to be offended.

41

"You getting some friends or are you turning into a lame dad?" Ashley laughed so hard she snorted.

"Oh my goodness. You two make me sick." He could hear Nicole in the background.

"I'll see you soon," Nasir said before hanging up.

I really do need a life.

10

Gary & Regina

egina sat at her home desk trying to plan out her week. She no longer worked for social services, so most of her days were spent trying to remain busy. Regina had enough money in the bank, so she truly didn't have to work another day in her life, but without a job, she felt useless.

Six months ago, Gary suggested she quit after noticing how stressed she was becoming. Ashley never returned to work after having the baby, something Nasir insisted on her doing despite her love for reuniting children with their families and finding them safe spaces. Ashley eventually agreed. She was ready to put all her focus into the child she birthed. Regina had already agreed to take over Ashley's caseload when she went on leave, but when she never came back the boss permanently assigned all those cases to her. All the overtime she was putting in was taking a toll on her body and Regina ended up in the hospital due to exhaustion. Gary was not happy.

Occasionally, Regina would still help her dad at the club, but only if she didn't have to deal with Shantel. Regina couldn't trust her if her life depended on it. At first, she was heartbroken, but as the months passed she began to heal. No big sister, no sister at all, should have to turn their back on their sibling, but Shantel's behavior was disgusting. Even if her relationship didn't work out with Gary, there was always the possibility of Shantel going after the next man that came into her life.

Regina spent months trying to figure out why Shantel hated her so much, but nothing came to mind. She came to the conclusion that was just the person her sister was and that would probably never change. Her dad hated that his daughters, who were once best friends, could barely stand to be in a room together. Shantel tried reaching out on numerous occasions to apologize, but when Regina didn't reply to any of those messages she eventually went back to being a spiteful brat.

"Babe, what you over there contemplating," Gary said walking over to Regina.

"Just trying to get my schedule written out. Trying to be productive you know?"

"And you do know that the point of you quitting your job was so you could spend some time relaxing." He placed his hand on her shoulders. "I was going to head out for a run, but how about we take a walk along the beach instead."

"No, maybe next time. Go get your workout in. It's Sunday, which means I need to get this place spotless. It's much easier to do that when you aren't around," Regina said, swirling around in her chair.

"What are you trying to say?" He asked leaning in.

"That you be coming over here dirtying up my place."

"If you'd just move in with me I wouldn't have to come over here at all."

"We've discussed this and I will not be moving into your place. You know how I feel about that?"

"Yeah, yeah. Until I put a ring on your finger and you carry my last name you won't be moving a thing into my place," Gary repeated Regina's previous response word-for-word.

Most women would have jumped at the idea of moving in with him, but not Regina, she was far too independent for that and she was still dealing with the trauma of losing the man she was supposed to marry. At times Gary felt he was in competition with a man no longer living and it ate away at his ego. Regina took down most of his pictures, but he was still very present in her home and her heart.

"I love you, but you have to let this whole moving-in conversation go."

"For now," he said kissing her on the forehead before turning her chair around. "I'll see you later. I'm going to head to the crib after my run."

Before Regina could respond Gary was out the door. She knew he was upset, but the conversation wasn't going to go anywhere he wanted it to. Regina was still in the process of healing and moving into his place wasn't going to magically fix the hole in her heart. Gary did all he could to help, but she needed to finish the job on her own.

"Okay, back to what I was doing," she said grabbing her pen.

Monday: *Meditate 30m - Journal 30m - Grocery Shopping 12:00 pm*

　　Tuesday: *Meditate 20m - Shadow Boxing 30m - Read 1hr Before Bed*

　　Wednesday: *Meditate 30m - Date w/ Gary 7:00 pm*

　　Thursday: *Meditate 30m - Journal 30m - Nighttime Yoga 7:00 pm*

Friday: *Therapy Session 9:00 am – Spa Treatment 11:00 am – Read before bed*

Saturday: *Braid Appointment 9:00 am – Bowling 8:00 pm*

Sunday: *Cleaning Day*

I need to take up a hobby, Regina thought as she looked at her plans. "I'll figure out something later."

Closing her planner, Regina made her way into the kitchen to put on a pot of coffee. Unlike most people who used those fancy pods, Regina enjoyed brewing her own. She was able to determine how strong she wanted it and she always had more to come back to later. Since she was already in the kitchen, that is where the cleaning would start, but first, she needed her music to get the energy right. The sink was full of dishes from the night before. Giving them a pre-wash, she loaded them into the dishwasher and pressed start. Spraying down the counters, she swayed her hips and sang along to Beyoncé as she wiped them down. After finishing up the kitchen, Regina lit some candles and decided to take a short break to enjoy the coffee she had put on.

Am I overthinking this whole moving-in thing, Regina thought as she sipped on her coffee. Gary hadn't done anything within their relationship for her to doubt how he felt, but he did have a past that couldn't be ignored. Regina didn't know if she had changed him for now or if their love was going to last always. She lost out on one love and she wasn't willing to risk losing another. If she moved in with Gary, she didn't want to have to look back.

"I need to meet up with the ladies this week," Regina blurted out as she jumped up to grab her phone. *Who better to talk to than Ashley and Rebecca?* she thought. They both moved in with their men within a year and although Ashley was no longer with Nasir, they still managed to get along, but then again they also had a baby.

> **Regina:** *Hey ladies! Let's make plans to meet up tomorrow. I want to talk to you about me and Gary. Let me know if this is doable for you both.*

Putting down her phone, Regina went back to dancing and cleaning her apartment. If anything was going to get her mind off her relationship, it was going to be a tidy apartment.

* * *

Sitting in his car, Gary wasn't sure where his relationship with Regina was going. There could be a possibility he wasn't the one she wanted to start life over with. If that was the case, Gary didn't know what he was going to do. The moment she opened her mouth to speak to him he knew that there was something there; something he had been afraid to explore with other women. Not because he wasn't ready, but because he had a fear of being hurt and left alone.

Now that he was ready to take the next step Regina wasn't. He feared that she wasn't as into him as he thought. The only way he was going to be able to get her into his home permanently was to marry her and though he was committed to his relationship, he didn't see marriage in their future...yet.

47

Being committed was a first for Gary, but he was getting a small glimpse into how he treated women in the past.

Gary noticed the look on Regina's face when Rebecca came walking down that aisle; the face of a woman who was supposed to already be married, but missed out on the chance due to a tragic accident. Maybe she felt like she wasn't going to get to that point with Gary by her side. The idea of not being able to be the one for Regina scared him, but what he feared more was losing out on the one woman that saw more than money when she looked at him. Regina saw Gary for who he truly was.

11

The Ladies

Ashley didn't know what to expect from her outing with Rebecca and Regina. Although Ashley talked to Rebecca here and there, they hadn't seen each other physically since her baby shower. *Will it be awkward? Will seeing her bring back all the hurt and pain I caused?* Ashley was feeling anxious, but she needed this. They could get the awkwardness out of the way and by the time the housewarming came around they would have already gotten through the weird stage.

The sun was shining bright and it was at least 80 degrees out, the perfect weather for Ashley to show off her new mom's body. She opted to wear a form-fitting, short-sleeved maxi dress that had a split going up the left leg, stopping just below the cup of her butt. Her hair was slicked up into a bun.

Ashley: *Hey ladies! I'll be heading out momentarily. Just had to get Little Nasir settled.*

Nicole agreed to babysit since Nasir had to go into the office and she had the day off from training. Any availability in her schedule typically went towards spending time with her nephew, especially since she was no longer dating. Derek attempted to reconcile with her, but Nicole was much smarter than that. He deliberately started treating her like shit so he could start another life with another woman much older than her and in the process, he managed to violate her physically. Being with him was a disaster waiting to happen and she was blessed enough to get out.

> **Rebecca:** *Also about to leave out. It's going to take me a little longer to get to you guys so I may be 10 minutes or so behind.*

> **Regina:** *See you ladies soon!*

The ladies agreed to meet between Calabasas and Downtown LA, so Rebecca wouldn't end up stuck in Monday's traffic.

"You look pretty," Nicole said walking into Ashley's room.

"I see you're still putting that key to use."

"Why to knock when I have the magic key," Nicole said jingling her keys in the air.

"You can at least announce yourself before you come in. One day you're going to scare me to death."

"If I do, just know that Junior is in great hands," Nicole responded. "Where is he by the way?"

"In his room napping, but he should be up in a second."

"Cool, I was thinking about taking him to see Nick."

"I don't know. Just have him come here."

"He has Ari all day and we were thinking we'd take them to the zoo. Nick hasn't got to spend much time with Junior and I know he misses him," Nicole said, trying to convince Ashley.

"That's not my fault. He can come over here anytime he wants."

"Now you know it's not that simple Ashley."

"But, it could be."

"Until Kim is comfortable around Nasir you have to put in some extra effort, not Nick."

"I hate this," Ashley said, making her way out of her room down to her sons'.

Going into the closet she grabbed his to-go bag and started filling it with extra clothes, diapers, wipes, and bids. Heading into the kitchen with the bag, she stuffed way more snacks and sippy cups than needed in it as well.

"I'm guessing I can take him," Nicole said following behind her.

"Yes, but you guys please be careful and do not let Nick give my baby any candy," Ashley said cutting her eyes at Nicole.

"Ashley, I got this. You just go and enjoy yourself."

"OK! Let me go grab my purse and kiss my baby goodbye."

* * *

About forty minutes after leaving home, Rebecca and Ashley both arrived at the rooftop. Spotting Rebecca, Ashley hesitated to get out of the car. Normally, she wasn't intimidated by anything, but the father of her son was still not over losing her to his best friend. It was only normal to feel some type of way.

"Get it together Ashley. We are here for Regina and that's it. Everything else is in the past," Ashley told herself. Looking into the mirror, she reapplied her lipstick and got out of the car.

"Hi, reservations for Regina Park."

"Right this way."

Whew, Regina is here, Ashley thought as she approached the table.

Their view was amazing. Looking up at the sky, the clouds were practically nonexistent and the waves from the ocean were extremely calming to watch. Rebecca looked stunning as usual, in a v-cut graphic T-shirt and distressed jeans. She wore her hair down; big and curly, which was very different from her typical straight ponytail. To Ashley's surprise, the voluminous hair made her features pop instead of hiding them.

Approaching the table. The ladies stood up and greeted Ashley with a hug. "Hey ladies, you look beautiful as always,"

"I'm so glad you two could make it. I needed someone to talk to about Gary and I consider both of you my best friends, so it was only right I could talk to you guys about it," Regina said sitting down.

"Don't tell me you two are breaking up," Ashley said.

"Or that he's back to his womanizing ways," Rebecca added.

"No, and he bet the fuck not be," Regina uttered.

Ashley and Rebecca glanced at each other, then back at Regina, "Then what is it?" They asked in unison.

"May I take you ladies' drink order?"

"Can we get a bottle of your best Rosé and if you could also bring out some calamari, extra crispy please," Regina requested.

"Anything else?"

"Could you bring us the lamb meatballs? They sound remarkable," Rebecca added.

"Personally, they're my favorite on the menu. I will get that bottle out to you ladies immediately," the waiter said before walking away.

"Long story short, Gary has been constantly asking me to move in with him, but I don't want to. I told him it was because I want to be married first, but to be truthful I don't think that's the real reason. I want to be married, but not yet."

"Gary asking you to move in is a big deal," Ashley replied. "All the years I've known him he has always had multiple women he involved himself with and he never took any of them seriously."

"I haven't known Gary as long as Ashley, but she's right," Rebecca added. "When I met him I couldn't even believe he and Brandon shared the same DNA. Seeing him with you is a different story. What's stopping you from wanting to move in?"

"Exactly what you too are talking about. I love Gary, it's true, but the man has a reputation."

"How long have you two been together?" Ashley asked.

"Bout as long as you've been living with Nasir and Rebecca with Brandon," Regina responded.

"Before you know it, it's going to be going on year three," Ashley said. "I don't think he has any plans of going back to his old ways."

"You might be right, but me moving in could change his mind."

"You not moving in could also change his mind. Did you think about that? You're afraid shacking up is going to change him, but you turning him down may make him think you don't see the relationship going any further," Rebecca added.

"You were with Nasir for two years and you guys never took that step," Regina countered.

"We spent so much time together it wasn't a thought and we worked a lot. I enjoyed coming home to my own space. I doubt he wanted to live with me and I damn sure didn't want to move into his place. We gave each other a drawer and called it a day," Rebecca laughed, "but with Brandon, as soon as he asked I packed my shit. I knew I never wanted to spend a day away from that man."

"You kept your apartment though," Regina responded.

"I sure did. I knew I wanted to be with him, but sometimes these men don't really want us. The apartment brought in extra income, but it was a safety net, especially after all the bullshit I'd been through with men. Once he proposed, I knew I didn't need it anymore. For me, it's all about having faith and I had an overwhelming amount in Brandon."

"I agree with Rebecca," Ashley chimed in. "You have to choose to be in or out. Our lives are already planned out by the man upstairs and he's just waiting for us to act on them. If Gary is going to go back to dealing with multiple women he is going to do that whether you live together or not. Besides don't you want to know what it's like living with a man before actually marrying him?"

"I tried that and he died."

"And that is not your fault," Ashley assured her. "The only person responsible for that unfortunate event is the drunk person behind the wheel that night."

"I've been trying to tell myself that for years," Regina said taking a sip from her glass.

"Until you find closure, you are never going to be hundred percent ready to commit to Gary," Rebecca spoke up. "Holding onto guilt and hurt fucks us up more than we like to admit."

"But, I'm not ready to forget him."

"Regina," Rebecca said as she reached out to hold her hand, "getting closure does not mean forgetting. You were in love with that man. You were going to be his wife. There is no way in hell you are going to forget him, nor should you. Hold all those beautiful memories you created close to your heart, but make some room."

"Whew, can you be my therapist," Ashley said wiping a tear from her face.

"I love you ladies," Regina said. "I appreciate this friendship and I hope we can do this more."

"I would love to," Rebecca replied.

"Me too," said Ashley.

"Well then, shall we make a toast to sisterhood?" Regina asked.

"Yes, let's make a toast to taking care of ourselves, building lasting bonds, and never letting dicks come between us chicks," Rebecca said raising her glass.

"Chicks before dicks," Regina and Ashley yelled out as their glasses kissed Rebecca's.

Once the ladies finished discussing Regina and Gary's situation. Rebecca and Ashley started discussing Brandon and Nasir's friendship. They needed to come up with a way to get the two of them in a room together. Like animals, they needed the men in a controlled environment; a place that wasn't too crowded or filled with strangers, but big enough to give them the space they needed to talk. Regina suggested everyone join in on bowling Saturday, but Rebecca and Ashley figured that would be too soon.

Ashley explained that she hadn't exactly told Nasir she'd been in contact with Rebecca for the last year. She admitted that she was afraid it would bring forth the anger he had suppressed. Their son was a huge distraction when it came to taking his mind off Rebecca and his past with Kim. Rebecca was still surprised by Nasir's aggressive side. She always knew he could be a little jealous, but she didn't know his anger went beyond that.

Because Brandon was already open to the idea of Ashley and Rebecca having a friendship, despite her dislike for him, Rebecca knew it would be easy to get him to agree to a meet-up. The real issue was figuring out how to convince Nasir. That's where Gary, Regina, and Ashley would come into play. Gary and Ashley have the longest and strongest relationship with Nasir. Gary being Little Nasir's godfather was also a plus.

The ladies thought it would be a great idea to get everyone out of town for a nice relaxing vacation. They'd rent a huge house in a secluded area with all the amenities everyone would need. They could bring groceries and plan daily meals. All they needed to do was figure out a date and location. Ideally, Ashley was hoping it could be before the housewarming, but a month would be too soon to plan the perfect getaway. She would have to find another way to break the news to Nasir about her and Rebecca's newfound friendship.

12

Rebecca

A pproaching her home, Rebecca was in awe. Since college, she'd been living in small dorm rooms and studio apartments. Thanks to Brandon, here she was living out her dreams, a dream she never thought she'd achieve. Their home sat on 4 acres of land. It was far enough to avoid disturbing the neighbors but close enough for emergencies. Anyone visiting would forget they were living in Southern California. The property gave contemporary ranch vibes, but without the barn, hay, and horses. There were 5 bedrooms, 6 bathrooms, a wine cellar, a library, an upstairs gym, and a heated outdoor pool.

As Rebecca pulled into the driveway and opened the 4-car garage, she spotted Brandon's. It was a quarter after four and she didn't expect him home until at least eight, but she had no complaints. Rebecca wanted to spend as much time with her husband as she could. In a fantasy world, the two of them would be off traveling the world, but this was reality and they had responsibilities. Rebecca needed to get back into her podcasting bag and manage a team of strong-minded women at the same time. Brandon promised that once they found the time they'd go on a romantic trip to, a place of her choosing. Until then Rebecca would be under her husband every chance she got.

Walking into the house, Rebecca was shocked to see the boxes gone. She planned to spend her week organizing the house, but from the looks of things, Brandon took care of it on his own. Rebecca loved how he managed to take the stress off of her without ever having to ask.

"Husband," Rebecca yelled out, "where are you and how did you get this house so spotless?"

"HUUUSSBEEEN," Rebecca yelled through the house, "come out come out wherever you are."

Rebecca was tipsy and it became clear to her when she started laughing hysterically. "Shh," she said putting her finger to her mouth.

Stumbling into their massive bedroom, she bumped right into Brandon. He had a towel wrapped around his waist and his body was all oiled up. "I told you to be quiet," she said smacking herself on the hand.

"Someone had a little too much fun," Brandon said holding onto Rebecca. "How much did you drink?"

"Just a few glasses." She laughed. "I promise I felt sober on the way back."

"Women and their wine," he said shaking his head.

"Yeah yeah, are you going to give your wife a kiss or am I going to have to take it?" She asked looking up. Without a word, he leaned down and kissed her like it was the first time. Kissing Brandon never got old.

"I'm one lucky woman." She blushed.

Pulling her in he said, "No, I'm the lucky one."

Standing on her tiptoes, Rebecca glided her hands to the back of Brandon's head and guided his lips to hers. Kissing him slowly, she parted his lips with her tongue and melted into him. "I love you," she said unwrapping his towel.

"I love you more."

Backing up she took in the beauty below his waste. Brandon had the prettiest dick she'd ever seen and she never missed out on admiring it, before proceeding to take care of business.

"You like what you see?" He asked, placing one hand on his hip and using the other to stroke his dick.

"Like," she said licking her lips, "I love it, enjoy it...I'm devoted to it."

"Well come show me then," he said swinging it around.

Standing a short distance away from Brandon, Rebecca slipped out of her shoes and began undressing, throwing away one item at a time until she was standing completely bare in front of her husband.

"Perfection," he said, looking her up and down. "Now bring all that goodness over here."

Dropping to her knees, Rebecca crawled over to Brandon, laughing at herself along the way, causing Brandon to burst out into laughter too. She was trying her best to remain sexy, but it was official, the Rosé came to play and it was winning.

"Don't laugh," she said looking up.

"Not laughing." Brandon lifted his head to the ceiling to hide the amusement on his face.

You won't be amused for long, she thought as she wrapped her mouth around his dick and brought it to the back of her throat. Brandon let out a groan and she hadn't even started working her tongue the way he liked. Rebecca's mouth felt like heaven and Brandon were enjoying every moment of it. He could barely stand, but Rebecca refused to let him move. She was devouring that man and the more he groaned the wetter she became.

"Jesus fucking Christ," Brandon screamed out as he came, letting off a load bigger than usual.

Rebecca swallowed every last drop and then licked him clean.

"Can I get a refill?" Rebecca asked wiping her mouth, "Or did I suck up all you had left?"

"You are something special," Brandon said lifting her off the floor. "I think I have a little extra something for my wife."

* * *

Brandon pleased Rebecca for hours. After her 5th and final climax, she went right to sleep. Brandon made his way downstairs to make dinner after taking another shower. He knew once Rebecca woke she'd be starving and the woman could eat. Shrimp and salmon were prepped and ready to go on the grill. He just needed to get the salad together. There was a bottle of Rebecca's favorite chardonnay in the fridge, but he figured they would save that for another night.

Before Rebecca arrived home wine-drunk, Brandon planned on having an intimate date night. He wanted to sit down with his wife for their first home-cooked meal in their forever home, which is why he came home early and hired an interior designer to get everything sorted. The process took longer than he expected, so once Rebecca got home it was too late to surprise her...at least the way he wanted to. Instead, she surprised him.

"Something smells good," Rebecca came walking into the kitchen, with a towel wrapped around her head and a T-shirt dress on. She sat down at the island in the kitchen and stared at Brandon as he plated their food. "Is this for me?"

"Who else would it be for? My imaginary friend?"

"Don't be an ass, but thank you," she said lifting herself over to grab the plate.

"Starved, I presume." He laughed, watching as she dug into the plate like an animal. "I was hoping we could share a romantic meal, but I see that'll have to wait."

"I'm sorry babe. Between you and the girls, I am worn out and feel like I haven't eaten in weeks. That shower helped."

Moving his plate next to Rebecca, he sat down to enjoy the food he cooked. Looking over, he couldn't believe hers was already half gone. "Speaking of the girls, how did that go?"

"It went well and as much as I hate to say it, the more I speak to Ashley the more I like her. She is sweet, but I do not know how she deals with Nasir. I'm sure she can find someone who doesn't act like such a brat or make her feel bad about speaking to certain people. You know he doesn't even know me and she speaks from time to time because she's scared of his reaction."

"Sounds about right, but if he doesn't know she speaks to you, how do you expect her to come to the house?" Brandon asked.

"First of all, she's a grown-ass woman who's currently single might I add. He can't and shouldn't control who she decides to be friends with. The man is going to have to get over it. Especially since we plan on seeing each other more."

"Oh, do you now?" Brandon asked, knowing if he tried to tell her otherwise he would be the one getting cussed out.

"I do. Do you have a problem with that husband?"

"Not at all, wife. As long as she doesn't come at you sideways it's all good on my end. I don't see a reason why we can't all be friends. We're adults right?"

"See, that's what we were saying," Rebecca said putting her

fork down, and turning to look at Brandon. "We think it's time you and Nasir make up."

Quietness took over the room. Rebecca had no clue what Brandon was thinking. It had been almost two years since the two of them communicated. The day he proposed to Rebecca was the day he decided he was going to let that friendship go for good. There was no way he could have both. Rebecca never tried to steer him away, in fact, she spent a lot of time advocating for their friendship to continue, but once Brandon had his mind made up it was quite hard to change.

"I thought we weren't going to have to deal with him being in our lives," Brandon finally spoke.

"We don't have to, but let's admit," she paused, "it would be a lot more convenient. Plus you two are practically brothers. Your real blood brother is still extremely close with him, being the god dad and all."

"That man needs to apologize for the way he treated you and me. Then maybe I'll think about letting him back into my life. Until then he's just somebody that I used to know," Brandon responded and went back to eating his food.

"Understood."

"So, that's why yo ass came home and sucked the soul from me," he said under his breath.

"No, I sucked the soul out of you because you're my husband and I wanted to," she snapped. "I can turn into a boring housewife if you'd like."

"Please don't," he begged.

"By the way...who came in here and took care of my wifely duties?"

"Some interior designers I hired. You should still be in vacation mode and not worry about having the house in order.

Not yet at least," he said leaning toward Rebecca. "Now give your husband a kiss please."

13

Ashley

U nlike the other ladies, Ashley remained sober. The one glass of wine she had barely pinched her. Ashley wanted to make sure she was good enough to make the drive back home and be fully alert for mommy duty. Nicole informed Ashley about bringing Junior back home so she didn't have to worry about stopping by her place to get him. Ashley was hoping his day out with his aunt and uncle wore him out, but anything was possible with that kid. He was always so full of energy.

Ashley: Hey ladies, I made it home! I had a great time. Let's do it again soon. Rebecca, please don't be a stranger.

Regina: The talk helped. Love you ladies and can't wait for us to meet up again.

Ashley sat her phone down on the counter and rushed to the room to shower, tearing her clothes off along the way. She wanted to freshen up before Nicole arrived with Little Nasir. Getting out of the house was exactly what she needed. Most days were spent teaching her son everything she could; social skills, communication, counting, colors, singing, and everything else under the sun. No longer working allowed her all the time in the world to spend with him, something she didn't get from her mother as a child.

Ashley took a quick shower, oiled up, and threw on a hoodie and boy shorts. As she sat at the edge of the bed, she could hear the garage door opening. *Shit*, she thought. Ashley hadn't told Nasir she was meeting up with Rebecca or Regina, which meant she also hadn't told him Nicole had their son today. Ashley rushed back into the kitchen to text Nicole to tell her not to mention anything about Rebecca.

"Where's my son?"

"Can I get a hi, a hello, how was your day?" Ashley said placing her hands on her hips.

"My bad," he said walking up and kissing her on the forehead. "How was your day today?"

"Thank you. My day went well. I just got home twenty minutes ago."

Ashley figured it would be best not to lie about going out in case Gary happened to say something to Nasir. The fact that she was the only single one in the group, but still had to lie to protect Nasir's feelings was beyond ridiculous. How would they ever be able to be more than friends if she couldn't even tell him the truth about her whereabouts?

"Oh," he replied, eyes wide, "where were you?"

"Regina was having some reservations about moving in with

Gary, so she wanted someone to talk to."

"How'd that go?"

"It went well. I think he might be getting a roommate sooner than later."

"I'm so proud of my guy. He's such an adult." Nasir smiled. "But back to my little man. Where is he?"

"Right here!" Nicole came strolling through the door with her nephew sound asleep in her arms.

"Where are you two coming from?" Nasir asked.

"Damn, can I go lay him in his bed before you start questioning me," Nicole said rolling her eyes and walking right passed Nasir. "He's had a busy day at the zoo."

"Sheesh, that's all you had to say."

"Maybe if you'd learn to start saying hi to people before interrogating them, they wouldn't get so defensive with you Mr. Wright," Ashley said turning away slightly.

"I'm working on it."

"You need to work a little harder." Nicole came back into the room flopping down on the couch.

"I'm guessing the kids wore you out." Ashley grinned.

"No, y'all son wore me out. That Ari is just as sweet as can be." Nicole grinned. "I adore her. She was so patient and attentive with Junior. You'd think he was her little brother."

"You went to the Zoo with Kim?"

Nasir looked at Ashley and then over at Nicole. They could tell he was agitated by the beads of sweat forming on his face and how he was rubbing the back of his neck aggressively.

"Would it be a problem if I had?" Nicole asked.

"No, she wasn't with Kim. Nick invited them to the Zoo and I said it was fine," Ashley quickly answered, biting her bottom lip.

Nicole hated how nervous her sister became at just the mention of Kim or Rebecca's name around Nasir. The moment they all found out about Nasir's violent past, Ashley's behavior changed drastically. She was more cautious of how she worded phrases, she rarely spoke up when Nasir was in the wrong, and she constantly made excuses for him. All she wanted to do was play peacemaker, but that wasn't going to fix his attitude.

"Come on Ashley. Even if Kim was with us it shouldn't be a problem. She's in our lives and isn't going anywhere. Nick is Juniors' uncle. When you had the baby, for a moment I thought everything would go back to normal but it's clear it isn't," Nicole said standing up. "I'm going to get out of here before the both of you ruin the beautiful day I had with my nephew and brother."

"I'll call you. Thanks again for today," Ashley responded, knowing she wouldn't be able to convince her to stay, let alone calm down. Nasir had officially pissed her off.

"When it comes to him, I'm *always* here to help," Nicole said as she walked out the door.

"Does she always have to get so upset?" Nasir asked, shaking his head. "I wasn't trying to be a jerk. I just wanted to know who my son was with."

"Nasir, do you think my siblings would ever let anything happen to our son?"

"No."

"Then maybe don't come off so confrontational next time. I wanted to hear how the day went. You know I'm still trying to get back on good terms with Nick."

"It's not like he isn't welcome here. He's the one who chooses not to come by."

"You beat up his girlfriend," Ashley blurted out in her

brother's defense.

"Wow. It was once. You act like I was just out there beating on women and I thought we were all past that," Nasir responded as if it made the situation any better.

Ashley couldn't believe how insensitive he was being, especially knowing the trauma she and her siblings endured throughout their lives. Instead of being able to be happy carefree kids, they had to constantly live in fear. That fear didn't stop when their mother passed away, they carried that trauma into adulthood. Ashley was sure Kim's experience changed her in some of the same ways. Ashley didn't know what to say to Nasir and she didn't have the patience to find the words.

"You can take care of our son for the rest of the night," Ashley said lowering her head and walking to the room.

Remembering her phone was charging on the kitchen counter, she got off the bed and made her way back to the living area. "Are you fucking kidding me?"

Nasir was standing in the kitchen trying to unlock her phone. The last time he looked at her messages she was pregnant and he had thrown it at her. She should have known then that he had issues. How was she going to help Rebecca repair his friendship with Brandon when it was obvious they needed to work through some issues of their own?

"We were doing so good Nasir," she said walking towards him and snatching the phone from his hand. "I want to be mad at you, but the only thing I am is disappointed. You need to seek some help and fix what's going on within you before you lose me for good and I take everything we agreed upon, which is a whole hell of a lot, with me."

Before he could respond, Ashley was back in her room and she didn't come out for the rest of the night, leaving him to handle all parental duties for the remainder of the night.

14

Nick

Nick hadn't gotten to spend as much time with Junior as he would have liked. Once he was born, everyone got along for a month or so then tensions formed again causing a slight divide. He was excited to be an uncle and was looking forward to spending all the time he could with him, but finding out what Nasir had done to the woman he fell for, changed the dynamic of their relationship.

Like Kim, who had put her trust in Nasir, Nick had done the same but for much longer. To find out a man he considered a brother put another woman through something he had to witness almost daily enraged him. He didn't mean for it to influence how he interacted with his sister and nephew, but Kim was just as special to him as they were. Imagine someone you love giving birth the same day you find out about a traumatic experience your significant other dealt with.

Kim tried her best to vocalize the importance of family and encourage Nick to keep taking steps towards repairing the ones he had, but every time she heard the name Nasir, her eyes told a different story. While most called his nephew Little Nasir,

Nicole and Nick took to calling him Junior, to help ease Kim's anxiety. Nick loved Nicole's support, especially because she wasn't much of a Kim fan. Her being older than Nick rubbed Nicole wrong. She was scared Kim might take advantage of him, but she proved to be solid.

While waiting for Kim to get home from work, Ari and Nick sat in the family room eating pizza and coloring unicorns. Ari was going on 6 years old but had the personality of a 60-year-old woman. Nick found it hilarious that she would use phrases like, "That's my cup of tea," "Back in my day," and "Kids these days," as if she wasn't a kid herself. At first, he thought she picked it up from her grandmother, but once Nick met her he realized she didn't speak in that manner either. As Nick put the finishing touches to his unicorn's tail, he could hear the door unlocking.

"Mommy's home from making that bacon." Ari jumped up and darted towards the door.

"Be careful my little angel. You don't want mommy to accidentally hit you with the door."

Stopping in her tracks, she placed her index finger on her chin and said, "You are absolute correct."

Nick chuckled knowing she meant to say absolutely. As Ari stood waiting to greet her mom, he picked up the coloring pencils and put them back into the storage box sitting next to him, then placed them on the coffee table. Picking up their plates of pizza, he quickly put them on the kitchen table before Kim could get in his ass about letting Ari eat in her living room.

"You forgot the towel," Kim said picking up Ari, to kiss her on the cheek. "My goodness you are one heavy girl."

"Must be all that yummy food I got to eat."

"And what yummy food was that?" Kim asked, putting down

Ari and closing the front door.

"That's our little secret," Nick said walking toward Kim.

"You better not have filled my baby up with a bunch of junk."

"Not a lot, just a little." Ari giggled and ran to her room.

"Pick out your PJs so you can get ready for a bath," Kim yelled behind her. "You two had a good day?"

"We did," Nick said taking Kim's bag and jacket. "She had a ball playing big sister to Junior. She'd make a great one. "

"Are you hinting at something?"

"Not yet. I'm enjoying the two ladies I already have, but one day," he said kissing Kim.

"Great, because we cannot afford to have another old soul walking around here. That girl is expensive," she replied, making her way down the hall to their bedroom.

Going into the bathroom, Kim hung her purse in the closet and then slipped off her shoes. She was ready to hop in a hot shower after dealing with clients and paperwork all day, but she still had one more little important client to take care of. Walking up behind her, Nick grabbed a hanger and placed her jacket on it so she could hang it as well.

"You won't have to worry much longer about handling finances solely. I'll be starting my new job soon and you won't be the only one bringing home the bacon."

Because of Nick's record, it had been difficult for him to find work, at least the work that he was interested in, but he wasn't giving up. The more time he spent with the twins he started asking about their production companies, the roles everyone played, and how he could get involved. Gary was willing to offer him an internship, but Nick needed a position that paid. Luckily Brandon was willing to help him out.

"Please don't start speaking like a person from the olden

days," Kim said placing her hand on Nick's shoulder.

"Looks like you caught the Ari bug too."

"So, when exactly are you going to be starting."

"Officially...next week, but he wants me to come in on Wednesday to meet everyone."

"I'm excited for you. I love how willing he is to get you back on your feet. Most people would look right passed someone with your record."

"Yeah, like you almost did." He smirked. "Was about to miss out on a good ass man 'cause you thought I was a little too hood."

"Sure was. I was not about to be playing nobody ride or die."

"MOM! I'M READY FOR MY BUBBLE BATH."

"HERE I COME!"

"While you get her bath together I'm going to get you one running as well," Nick said smacking Kim on the ass.

"You might want to hold off on that for at least 30 minutes. You know how she is."

"You're right, get her settled so I can cater to you."

"You can start by cleaning up the rest of that mess in the living room. Please and thank you," she replied before exiting the room.

15

Gary & Nasir

"Pretty sure Ashley wants me to go to therapy," Nasir said bent over and trying to catch his breath

"Done already?" Gary said jogging in place next to him in an attempt to avoid the conversation that was about to ensue. "You getting old."

"Did you hear what I said?"

"Yeah yeah, I heard you. I didn't know we came out here to vent about our women. It's too early in the morning."

When Nasir woke up, he hit Gary to go for an early morning run before work. Typically he would run around the neighborhood and then return home for his smoothie and a shower. Today, he thought it best to pack up his bag so he could shower and change at his office since Ashley was still upset.

"Well damn, I thought I could at least bring it up to my brother."

"That was you and Brandon's thing, but let me try this whole brotherly advice thing out." Gary stopped jogging in place and began to stretch before getting into a serious conversation with Nasir. He wasn't completely sure what Nasir wanted to hear, but what Gary had to say he most likely wouldn't like. Ashley was right, Nasir needed to talk to somebody and Gary was not qualified to heal what Nasir had going on inside. A therapist was probably his best bet.

"So, what's going on? I thought the two of you were on good terms and whatnot."

"We have been, but she caught me attempting to get into her phone," Nasir answered nonchalantly.

"Nigga what? What reason do you have to be all up in that woman's phone? Are y'all back together?" Gary asked scratching his head. "Matter a fact, don't even answer that because even if y'all were, there's no reason for you to be going through her shit." The last thing Gary would get caught doing is going through his woman's phone. That's a sure way to put your insecurities on display and let your woman know you don't trust her. "When you trust someone, you don't go looking for answers you don't want."

"I don't know what got into me. I haven't been through her phone since that mess went down with Shantel, but when I got home and my son wasn't there I got a little suspicious."

"Nigga suspicious of what? You the one being weird," Gary said shaking his head. "Ashley has nothing to hide from you. If anything she's walking on eggshells around you and you're too stupid to even notice."

"What do you mean walking on eggshells?"

"Exactly what I said. Every move she makes, she makes with you in mind. She won't speak on certain topics or people because she doesn't want to put any cracks in the foundation you two are building. I don't know how you can't see that, but everyone else around can. If she wants you to go to therapy just do it. If not, move out of that house *you* bought and on with your life."

"Would you go to therapy for Regina?"

"Of course, I would, but I don't need therapy. I know what my problem is. Do you?" Gary questioned. "From the look on your face, I can tell you don't."

* * *

Nasir pulled into the private parking lot of his office and parked his car in his designated spot. His name was plastered in huge font. Ashley hated seeing it whenever she went to visit his office. There was no reason to have it there except to show everyone who the boss was. Leaning his sit back, Nasir closed his eyes for a few seconds and thought about what Gary had said to him. *Why am I so hostile at the mention of any of those people's names? I don't have a reason to be angry.* Before Nasir got too deep in his thoughts he was startled by a knock on his window.

"Hey, boss man. What are you doing there?"

Standing there was Nasir's top agent, Emery, with a cup of coffee in her hand. Emery was a tall slender woman with long, bouncy, blonde hair that she flipped every chance she got, especially when she had good news. Emery had been working for Nasir for six months and she was doing better than most of the agents that had been working beside him for years. Nasir loved how she always had ideas to bring in more buyers, lively up showings, and expand their reach beyond the Los Angeles area. Emery was usually the first in the office and always the last to leave.

Jolting himself upright, Nasir turned off the car and popped his trunk, prompting Emery to take a step back so he could open the car door.

"Good morning Emery. You're in early," he said closing the door behind him and making his way to his trunk to grab his change of clothes.

"I could say the same about you." She followed closely behind him. "If I knew you'd be here this early I would have grabbed you some coffee as well."

"Oh, that's alright. I'm not much of a coffee person. I prefer to have my green drinks."

"That explains why you look toned and lean." Emery smiled awkwardly.

"That and my daily runs," Nasir said closing his trunk. "Should we go inside now?"

"I'll lead the way," Emery said prancing towards the door to put in the security code.

Emery settled into her work area to begin going over contracts, and current, and new listings. Nasir left her to work and headed to the men's bathroom, which was more like a spare bedroom/bathroom in a house. Since a lot of the agents spent 80% of their time in the office he wanted to make sure everyone felt at home. While in the shower, Nasir couldn't stop thinking about what Ashley, Nicole, and Gary had said to him. It was becoming extremely clear he was the common denominator in every problem, going back to his breakup with Ashley back in college. Even in his relationship with Rebecca, if something didn't go slightly his way, there was an issue. If Nasir didn't get it together, Ashley was going to take him for all she could. *I'm such a dumbass for coming up with that agreement*, he thought, *we aren't even married.*

Stepping out of the shower, Nasir grabbed his phone and texted Gary.

Nasir: *You know any good therapist, preferably a black one?*

16

Monica & Nikki

Nikki sat at her desk with her eyes closed and her head toward the ceiling. Her heart was racing and her legs shaking. Nikki was on the verge of climaxing and there was nothing she could do to stop it. As Monica nibbled and sucked on her clit, waves rushed through her.

"Jesus Christ," Nikki moaned out, "I'm going to cum."

Monica squeezed onto her thighs to spread her legs wider, diving her tongue into Nikki's nectar. Monica loved the taste of her on her tongue and hearing the sound of pleasure escape her lips. It made her feel powerful.

Monica lifted her head from under the desk and positioned herself face-level with Nikki. "Ain't nothing like a good breakfast in the morning."

"Let me taste," Nikki said licking Monica's lips and parting them with her tongue. They lingered in a passionate kiss for several minutes before being disturbed by the sound of Monica's phone.

"I love to watch you cum," Monica said standing up.

"And I hate to see you go." Nikki grazed her lips.

Monica's agent was waiting for her outside of the building. If she had to wait any longer, Monica would be finding her way around for the day. Today her agent agreed to accompany her to a photo shoot for a bathing suit line and then immediately after they needed to go meet with the producer of the new television show she'd possibly be a part of.

"I'll be back before you know. Keep my cushion warm," Monica said leaning down to kiss Nikki, placing a finger into her honeypot.

"Don't tease me or you'll be missing that meeting." Nikki quivered from the strokes Monica was giving.

"I just needed one more taste," Monica said sucking the finger she just removed from Nikki. "I love you."

"I love you too!"

Monica was out the door and Nikki needed to try to get back to the book she was supposed to be writing, but first, she went to the bathroom to clean the leftover juices from between her thighs. Getting up she realized she had come all over her leather chair. *And that's exactly why I tell everyone leather is best*, she thought looking down at the mess she made, *easy clean up.* Sitting back down in her now sanitized chair, Nikki opened up her word doc and glared at the blank screen, hoping words would magically appear.

Since moving in with Monica, she had been experiencing writer's block, which was a first for her. If anything she thought it would spark a story idea on top of a story idea. Instead, she found herself distracted by Monica's newfound career and mind-blowing sex, which she could have been writing about but she wanted to take her career in a new direction. Nikki was known for being an erotic author, but she wanted to branch out of that field into romance, maybe even thrillers.

The book she released with Rebecca had been on the best-seller's list for months and thanks to the podcast they created she was gaining a wider fan base. This was the time to keep building off that momentum and she figured a new book would do the trick, but no matter how many times she pulled out her laptop nothing came to mind. Writing a novel with multiple twists and turns was much harder than it seemed and took way more imagination than a book about people fucking almost every page. If she couldn't come up with something soon, the advance she received from the publication would need to be returned. Nikki could afford to pay it back, but she'd much rather keep her bank account stacked.

Pulling out her notebook, Nikki began jotting down ideas.

Ideas For New Book

1. Lovers Turned Enemies
2. Sisters w/ a Deadly Secret
3. Husband Sleeping w/ Brother-n-Law
4. Small Town Romance
5. ~~Fell For Exes Best Friend~~
6. ~~Secretly in Love w/ A Close Friend~~

"One of these has to work," Nikki said looking down at her notebook, crossing out the ones that resembled too closely to her friends' lives.

"Just start writing Nikki. You can do this!"

Natalie sat on the floor of the garage while the car remained running. How would her sister ever forgive her for running down the man she was supposed to be marrying in two weeks? "I'd rather die than tell her the truth," Natalie said crying. She wasn't even sure if she had killed him or not. Hopefully, the woman he was with didn't see me, she thought.

"Hmm, this could work," Nikki said tapping her fingers together with excitement as she looked at the words on her laptop screen.

* * *

Filming hadn't started yet, but Brandon insisted everyone come into the studio to meet each other. This was his first time producing a television show, but he wanted everyone involved to feel like they were part of a family. For his production to run smoothly he needed everyone as comfortable as possible.

Walking into the dimly lit building, there were boxes of equipment sitting off to the side, and a group of stagehands setting up the main stage with props and lights. Most of the scenes would be shot onsite at the main female character's "house", but Brandon wanted to make sure everything was staged, that way when the actors and actresses came in everything would be ready to go.

"Is Brandon around?" Monica asked one of the guys walking towards the back with coffee. As he turned around she realized it was Nick. "Hey! What are you doing here?"

"Just helping Brandon out, coming to meet everyone before it starts getting crazy around here. Come this way." Nick waved her over as he started to make his way down a long hall with rooms named after famous sitcom actors and shows.

"I wasn't supposed to come in until tomorrow, but Brandon set up this last-minute get-together and thought I should be here," Nick continued.

"Looks like we just may be working together. I needed to come in and settle a few more things before signing my paperwork."

"He's right in there," Nick said pointing in the direction of Brandon's office. "Hope to see you around."

17

A Session With Regina

Regina sat across from her therapist on a white curved sofa, which sat in front of a wall of books with topics ranging from death, healing, forgiveness, mental health, and more. On each end of the couch sat two small square side tables that stayed decorated with white floors, a eucalyptus candle, and boxes of tissues for those clients who couldn't control their tears. Regina had gotten through her crying phase, though Dr. Bell had a way of making her shed a tear now and then; sometimes tears of joy other times tears of pure sadness.

"I know he isn't coming back, obviously, but I feel like a horrible person for moving on. I vowed to never love anyone else and I broke that promise." Regina squeezed the black pillow that was sitting on her lap.

"Do you believe David would want you to spend the rest of your life sitting at home wishing he hadn't died or would he want you to live out your dreams of becoming a wife and a mother?" Dr. Bell sat with her legs crossed, patiently waiting for Regina to answer her question.

Regina had been seeing Dr. Bell on and off for about four years, but her visits had become more frequent after the fight with Shantel. Her bringing up David during their argument sent her over the edge and back into a place of hurt, doubt, and anger. She tried her best to hide it from Gary, but then he started talking about them sharing a living space and it was too much for her to handle on her own.

"My happiness meant everything to David. I know for a fact he'd want me to live my life to the fullest. He would want me to explore the world, try new hobbies, and meet new people," Regina answered.

"And I'm assuming falling in love again would fall in line with meeting new people, right?"

"I assume," Regina said.

"So what's truly holding you back when it comes to the current man in your life?" Dr. Bell sat her notebook down on the coffee table separating the two of them and picked up her mug, sipping it slowly. "Could it be you're afraid of losing Gary the way you lost David or could it be you don't see this making it to the chapel and beyond?"

Five minutes had passed and Regina had yet to answer any of Dr. Bell's questions. Instead, she looked off in the distance out the window, contemplating her answer, but it was clear to Dr. Bell she didn't have one.

"You don't have to answer now, but next time we meet I'd like one or something close. If possible, I would like to see both of you in my office. I find couple sessions to be very helpful and I can get a feel of what Gary is like when you two have these deep discussions."

"I'm not sure he'd come."

"If he loves you like you say he does he will come," Dr. Bell assured her. "Let's get that set up two weeks from now so we don't forget about it and that will also give him time to decide if therapy is something for him."

"Sounds like a plan," Regina answered.

"Your sister—" Dr. Bell started to speak but was cut off by Regina.

"What about my sister? As far as I'm concerned she doesn't exist," Regina said folding her arms.

"What would happen if one day she didn't exist? If you lost her the way you lost David? How would you feel?"

"I'd be fine," Regina said, looking away.

"Are you positive about that or are you just upset still?"

"Obviously I'm upset," Regina turned back towards Dr. Bell. "She's a bitch and she needs to learn how to live a life that doesn't include me."

"It's clear you aren't ready to forgive and I won't push the topic," Dr. Bell paused, "but remember, you and David weren't on the best of terms before his passing and it still eats away at you. I know Shantel hurt you, but you two share the same blood. I'm not telling you she was right in her actions, but you are the last person I want to see walking around filled with regret. Our time is up, but I want you to continue writing down your feelings and talking to that wonderful man of yours. I'll see you next week at the same time."

"See you next time."

18

Rebecca

Thanks to a good meal, good dick, and great sleep, Rebecca woke up feeling energized and ready to start the day. Looking over to her right, a smile formed on her face. She was still in disbelief that the man lying next to her was her husband. By now, she'd usually be sick of any other man, but this one was everything to her. The love she so desperately yearned for was being shown to her in new ways every day; it was unconditional and hers for a lifetime.

Brandon was sound asleep. Rebecca gazed at him for a short period, admiring his thick black eyebrows, the mole-like freckles starting to form on his smooth face, and his lips that poked out more than usual during his sleep. She was tempted to kiss them but didn't want to wake him. The clock read 5:00 a.m. meaning he would be sleeping for at least two more hours. He didn't need to be at the studio until about 9:00 a.m. Despite living with Rebecca for years, he hadn't gotten used to her early morning schedule, but she liked it that way. It allowed her time to reflect and spend quality time with herself.

Thinking about what she could get into for the day, it had

dawned on her that she hadn't filmed an episode of Rebecca Loves A Read. *That will be on the agenda for the day,* she thought as she quietly slipped out of the bed. Her new home library would be the perfect place to film, but before that, she wanted to get a good workout in to start the day. This would be her first time breaking into their home gym, which Brandon had completely set up with Rebecca in mind. There was also an indoor sauna that Rebecca would be putting to use every chance she got. Walking into her closet, Rebecca slipped into her workout leggings and sports bra. Exiting the room, she went into the guest room to wash her face and brush her teeth. Rebecca wanted to avoid making too much noise.

By the time she finished her workout, she was drenched in sweat from head to toe. If she attempted to get in the Sauna she'd pass out from dehydration. As Rebecca wiped the sweat off her face, Brandon appeared in the mirror and he had a smoothie in his hand.

"Good morning wife," he said walking up behind her. "I would hug you, but I'm over here looking fly and I'd hate for your sweat to get all over my suit," he said kissing the spot of her forehead that had just been cleared of sweat.

"Good morning husband. This is exactly what I needed or I was going to pass out."

"How long have you been in here?"

"What time is it?" Rebecca asked.

"7:30."

"Whew, I've been in here for almost two hours. Thought I'd break in the equipment."

"And you look damn good doing it. I wanted to come in here before I get into that traffic. I'll be home at the usual time tonight. Let me know if you want me to bring anything back,"

Brandon said kissing his wife one more time before heading out.

"I love you, Mr. Young," Rebecca said blowing a kiss.

"And a love you a million times more," Brandon said catching her kiss and pretending to put it in his pocket.

* * *

"Hello everyone and welcome to another episode of Rebecca Loves A Read."

Rebecca had her camera set up facing the reading nook that looked out towards the greenery, which was the backdrop of their home. It could be seen from almost every room. Each wall was lined with books, sorted by the colors of the rainbow.

"I know it's been a while since you've heard from me, but a bitch was off somewhere beautiful getting married to the man of my dreams. Yes, ladies, I'm officially Mrs. Young," Rebecca said showing off her upgraded ring. "It's stunning right? Well, wait until I get my wedding pictures. I will be creating a video with some exclusive footage from the start of planning up until the day we moved into our brand new home."

Rebecca had so much good news to share with her audience, but she couldn't do it all in one sitting. She was looking forward to filming and reconnecting with her internet family. She would be busy helping run the publication, but she would find time around that and being a wife to get back to her passion.

"Yes, we bought a new home as well. We haven't had a housewarming yet, but once we get to share our home with our loved ones, you all will be next. This room is going to be my sanctuary," Rebecca said, taking the camera off the tripod to give a 360 view of her library. The room was every book lover's dream. Never in a million years did she think she would have her library. All she could think about was the many books she'd be spending her hard-earned money on.

"Be sure to subscribe to my channel and my newsletter to stay updated on all things Rebecca," she said placing the camera back onto the tripod.

"Now, onto the topic of the day," Rebecca said adjusting herself to a more comfortable position, "Friendship and Forgiveness. Recently, I reconnected with a childhood friend of mine thanks to my wonderful husband. Me and this friend gradually stopped speaking to each other and then suddenly one day he completely vanished from my life. I was devastated and I went through every emotion known to man. First I remember being confused, wondering why he wouldn't pick up my calls or answer my text. What did I do to make him disappear on a decades friendship? Then those feelings turned to sadness and rage. I eventually got to the point where I no longer thought about him, except for when my mother would ask about him or a random song or movie we enjoyed came on." Rebecca smiled at the thought. "I guess my husband, who was my fiance at the time, noticed I still missed my best friend despite the effort I put into forgetting him. If it weren't for him I don't know if I would have ever talked to my best friend again."

After recording for almost an hour, Rebecca ended her video with these words.

"When the people we love most and share the most memories with hurt us, our reaction to being hurt can go to extreme levels causing those relationships to end. Our pride gets in the way and we train our brains to hold those grudges dear to our hearts. We get to a point where we refuse to relight the friendship flame, even when our hearts are aching to have them near us. Many of us, including myself, have to work on putting our pride and egos to the side. Life is too short and once we transition into the place unknown, whether that be heaven or some other universe, there's no get back. "

Once editing was finished, Rebecca uploaded her video for the world to see. Secretly she was hoping Nasir would watch as well. It was her way of helping move her plan with the ladies along.

"Now what should I do with the rest of my Friday?"

19

"Couples" Bowling

"Y'all ready to get y'all asses beat in this here game," Gary said, stretching like he was getting ready to run a marathon.

"Babe, you not even that good."

"Wanna bet?"

"I bet the only ass getting beat tonight is yours," Regina said while making a smacking gesture.

"Too bad none of you are going to be leading on the board," Ashley chimed in.

"Since when are you a pro at bowling? Last time I remember bowling with you, we had to turn on the bumpers because you had a fit about not being able to knock any pins down." Gary chuckled.

"Wow, we were like 14," Ashley said cutting her eyes at Gary, "I've improved."

As teenagers, the guys and Ashley spent a lot of time at the bowling alley after football games or any free day they had. The sounds of bowling balls hitting the floor, music throughout the building, children running, and people cheering whenever all

10 pins went falling, always made Ashley feel safe. When Ashley was in a bowling alley she knew that she could be a kid again and not have to worry about the dysfunction waiting for her back home.

"Still counts," he responded.

"I wish Brandon was here. You wouldn't be talking all that mess," Ashley uttered.

"You always thought he was the better twin." Gary shook his head.

"Honestly, you both suck, but yeah I liked him a little more," Ashley admitted.

Ashley could see the look on Nasir's face, he didn't want to partake in any conversation about Brandon, let alone think about him. This was the second time this week someone had mentioned his name. If he heard it one more time, the next logical thing was for him to appear. Not wanting to be the downer of the group, Nasir inserted himself into the trash talk.

"Y'all doing all this talking, but let's see if y'all really about something."

Still annoyed with him, Ashley sighed and said, "Wasn't nobody talking to you."

"Burn," Gary said touching Ashley's shoulder and following up with a sizzling sound effect.

"Why are you so annoying?" She asked. "Nevermind, don't answer that."

"Guys against girls?" Regina asked as everyone made their way toward the counter, hoping to clear the tension between Ashley and Nasir.

An attendant around the age of seventeen, stood behind the counter heavily spraying the shoes that had been left behind on the countertop. It was a surprise he hadn't passed out the way he hadn't taken his hand off the trigger of the spray can.

Glad I brought my shoes, Ashley thought as they approached him.

"Yeah, that way we don't have to share a lane with anyone," Ashley answered.

"How many of you will be bowling tonight?" The attendant asked looking up at them.

"Four," Regina answered, "and we'd like two lanes if possible. We're going to have a little friendly competition."

"Sounds fun. How many games?"

"Two should be fine," she replied.

Once they received their shoes and lane numbers, Ashley and Regina went to sit their belongings down so they could go searching for the perfect ball. They needed something light enough to hold comfortably, smooth enough to glide down the lane with ease, but heavy enough to send the pins crashing. There was a science to bowling, one that Ashley wasn't sure she figured out yet, but she wasn't going to let the guys know that.

"I'm going to put you and Ashley on the same team," Gary said entering their names in the machine.

"Dude, that woman barely wants to talk to me. She has had me watching our son as if I were a single parent. That's how I know she's pissed. That woman rarely lets him out of her sight, so what makes you think she wants to be on my team?"

"What better way to get her talking? She used to love this shit when we were kids and it might get you back on her good side," Gary insisted. "By the way did you set up that appointment with the therapist?"

"Yeah, but I haven't brought it up to Ash yet."

"Well look there," Gary smirked, "this might be the perfect time to thank Regina for referring you. Say it loud enough for

Ashley's ass to hear. You'll score a point on her board most def." Gary winked.

"You always got tricks up your sleeve."

"Only for the woman I want to keep," he said glaring over at Regina, who was giggling with Ashley about who knows what. Gary noticed she was in a better mode after her therapy session the day before. She said she needed to talk to him about something but they hadn't gotten around to it yet.

"Ugh, why am I on his team?" Ashley slightly yelled when she looked up at the screen.

Nudging her, Regina whispered, "The plan," and then grinned.

I wish I could say fuck that plan, she thought as she sat her ball down.

"Once upon of time, you used to beg to be on my team. I guess you don't like me like that anymore." Nasir pouted.

"Don't be such a baby," Ashley replied.

"Sounds like we got that all worked out. So first love versus new love. May the best team win," Gary said wrapping his arm over Regina.

"Can you go grab us some drinks first?" Regina asked, but Gary knew it was a demand. "Thank you, Daddy," she said knowing it would boost Gary's ego.

"Go help," Ashley said pushing Nasir in the direction of the bar.

"Sheesh, why can't you be nice and sweet like Re-"

"Like who?" Ashley interrupted Nasir before he could finish his sentence.

"No one sweetie. I love you just the way you are." he winked at Ashley and then proceeded to walk away.

"He's such a kiss ass," Ashley said sitting down to put on her shoes.

"But you love it."

"I love him, but I need a change to come. I can't keep holding onto childhood fairy tales and ignoring the fact that he and my siblings are not coexisting the way I expected."

"Between me and you," Regina said looking towards the bar and then back to Ashley, "I referred him to my therapist. He asked Gary if he knew of one, so he gave him mine."

Ashley's doe eyes widened and her eyebrows arched. She was shocked that Nasir was looking for a therapist. She had told him to seek help, but she didn't think he'd actually do it. *Maybe there is hope for us*, she thought.

"Male or female?"

"Female."

"Is she any good?"

"Do you think I'd be seeing her if she weren't? I've been going to her for at least four years now and she hasn't steered me wrong. She doesn't sugarcoat and if you come in being half truthful, she'll spot it quickly. As long as he puts in the work it'll be beneficial for him," Regina responded.

"What's her name? I trust your word, but I want to look her up as well. Maybe she could be of help to me."

"Her name is Dr. Bell," Regina hesitated, "Dr. Olivia Bell."

"Thank you," Ashley said writing the name down in her notes.

"Ready to get y'all asses kicked," Gary said as he and Nasir approached with two pitchers full of Margaritas.

"You act like we're at the club," Ashley laughed. "Really? Two?"

"Hey! What's wrong with the club? That's where I met this lovely lady."

"And you haven't been back since," Nasir added.

"Sprung!" Nasir and Ashley said at the same time.

"I sure am," Gary said putting down the drink. He snatched Regina up by the waist and they tongued down each other in the nastiest way possible.

"That used to be us," Nasir smirked.

"We couldn't have been that disgusting." Ashley scrunched up her nose.

"You might be right," Nasir responded as he watched Gary grope Regina. It looked like he was just moments away from ripping off her clothing. "OK OK, that's enough. Can we get to the game?"

"PLEASE!" Ashley insisted.

20

Gary & Regina

"Your best friends should be there for you through the hard times as well as the good ones. They should be there supporting you on the new journeys you venture, the children you bare, during times you think your world is going to end, and those moment's that completely take your life in a new direction...a positive one. I couldn't imagine making it through my wedding day without my best friends beside me. I'm blessed to have known them since childhood because most people don't get to experience that. If you and a friend you've known for decades are on the outs, it's worth it to try to work things out if you haven't already. "

Ashley: That girl is good...

Regina: Girl what the hell are you talking about?

Ashley: Rebecca posted a new vlog on her channel. I'm surprised you didn't get the notification.

Regina: I haven't looked at my email. I'm going to go watch it now.

Regina put down her phone and went to go grab her laptop from her bookshelf. Opening her email, she typed in Rebecca and the notification for her new video appeared. She opened it and began watching. It was an hour long, but Regina had nothing better to do than clean up once again. The days just seemed to fly by now that she was a "retired" woman.

"What have you so tuned in." Gary walked into the room.

Per usual, he stayed the night with Regina as he had done almost every Saturday night. After bowling, he planned to drop her off at home, but Regina begged him to come inside and no part of him wanted to pretend he didn't want to be there. They talked, made love, and then talked some more. Regina brought up the idea of couple's therapy and he agreed. Gary was relieved.

"Just about to watch one of Rebecca's videos about friendship and forgiveness."

"Mind if I pull up a chair? Maybe I can learn a thing or two."

"Go for it," Regina said pressing play. Once the video ended she texted back Ashley.

Regina: I knew that woman was smart LOL. Now it's time for me to do my part. I hope you're being nice to Nasir.

"If I'm not mistaken," Gary paused and turned slightly so he could look Regina in her beautiful eyes, "could she be hinting at Brandon and Nasir's friendship."

"I knew all those women were wrong." Regina grinned slightly.

"Wrong about what?

"You being a dumb ass." She burst into laughter.

"Thanks a lot, babe." He cut his eyes at her. "So I'm right? She wants them to be friends again?"

"Obviously. Do you know how awkward it is for us to have to hang out with each of them separately and for Ashley to be sneaking around with Rebecca?"

"Sneaking around you say?" Gary's eyebrows raised.

"Don't be a perv," Regina said hitting his chest, "they're friends."

"Does Brandon know this?"

"Yes, the only person who doesn't know is your buddy Nasir."

"I'll see what I can do. I need to speak to my brother first though."

"I honestly think he's fine with it, but how about we do a double date or something? He always gives in when it comes to Rebecca."

"That's the reason we're in this awkward situation now," Gary said standing up.

"Well, they are married now. Nasir is just gonna have to let it go. I think he still wants to be with Ashley anyway. They're just in a rough spot at the moment and if you ask me, he's being difficult just to be difficult."

* * *

Gary: *Did you see Rebecca's Read?*

Nasir was sitting in the rocking chair in Little Nasir's room reading him a book when his phone buzzed in his pocket. The first word that he registered was Rebecca's name. Nasir hadn't watched any of her videos in almost two years. Watching her with his best friend or ex-best friend in a bathtub together made his stomach churn and him jealous. He and Rebecca had never gotten that intimate or shared any part of their romance with the world in the way they had. To him it was so very obvious they were meant for each other, but he wished it could have been anyone but Brandon. Nasir hadn't prepared to lose his woman and his friend within months of each other.

Nasir: *I unsubscribed. Why?*

Gary: *Oh, no reason. Just wondering.*

Nasir: *You do know you're a terrible liar right?*

Gary: *That's not what your mama said.*

Nasir: *Nigga don't make me come to Regina's house and slap you.*

Gary: *Man, you ain't gon' do shit. Just go on her page and hit me later.*

"Dad...Dad, book." Little Nasir was tapping at the book sitting on his dad's lap *If You Give A Mouse A Cookie.* His mom used to read it to him all the time when he was a kid and now he was doing the same with his son.

"My bad son," Nasir said rubbing his curly hair and readjusting him in the seat. "You getting heavy boy."

Little Nasir laughed as if his dad just told a funny joke, which made Nasir laugh along with him. Ashley could hear the two of them. Her son's tiny voice sounded like heaven to her ears and it brought her a joy she didn't even know existed. She once depended on Nasir as a young woman to give her those feelings, but becoming a mother replaced that. She wondered why her mother couldn't love her that much as she watched Nasir be loving, kind, and patient. They were made to be parents and she was glad she had the chance to do it with him.

"Mommy!"

Nasir looked over at Ashley standing in the doorway. She looked like a ray of sunshine. The cloud that had been hanging over her disappeared. He knew he was making the right decision by attending therapy. It would be a shame for her to lose that glow because he had no self-control. Ashley deserved way more than just the financial stability he was providing; the world is what she deserved, unlimited love and respect is what she deserved, and he was ready to be the one to provide it to her again. There was no reason for him to check for what Rebecca had to say. He had all he needed right before him.

"Come join us."

21

Rebecca

"Good morning Sunshine."

"Good morning," Laura said walking into Rebecca's office. "I wasn't expecting you back so soon."

"If I could have laid up in bed for another week, trust me I would have, but duty calls, and Brandon started shooting a pilot for a new series."

"Ooo, sounds like an exciting job."

"It should be. He is working on his first rom-com. It's going to be about two best friends who eventually fall in love. You know the typical trope, but this time it's going to be a black cast and none of that stereotypical drama. Monica is actually going to be one of the main characters."

"Well, I can't wait to watch! It's good to have you back in the office. These people in the design department have been driving me crazy. They refuse to listen to anything I say, and then get pissed off when they have to start something over," Laura said shaking her head.

"It's because these women around here do not want to take orders from anyone younger than them, especially someone as young and beautiful as you." Rebecca smiled.

When Diane decided she wanted Rebecca to be part owner of the company that gave her the power to promote and hire who she wanted. With that power, she gave Laura a hefty raise and promoted her to head of the design department. Most of the designers were in their mid to late thirties, but Laura was a fresh 21. Almost everyone complained about her not having as much experience as they did, which was true, but Laura brought life into their company. Diane's main intention for bringing in a young designer was for a fresh perspective and that was everything Laura had, plus she was just as talented, organized, and confident as someone who had been running a company for ages.

"Ever since you promoted me them cougars been coming for my head. I've been keeping myself cool, but I'm ready to snap, especially on that damn Vicky."

"Is she becoming a bigger problem than she already is?" Rebecca asked.

"So you know how we are working on that book cover for Ann Reid?"

"The thriller about the twin sister and her creepy brother-in-law? Yes, how could I forget?" Rebecca said cringing because she knew how that story ended.

"Yes, that one."

"What about it?"

"Vicky took it upon herself to change the design completely and then present it to Ann. She was threatening to pull the whole book and take us to court over it," Laura revealed.

"What the fuck? Why didn't anyone tell me about this? I can't wait to talk to her. This is not the first time she's done some stupid shit like this. What did Diane say?" Rebecca was now rambling on with anger.

"Take a breather," Laura said, finally taking a seat at Rebecca's desk.

"We didn't say anything to you because you were away on your wedding/honeymoon and then Kim had told me you guys would be getting settled into the new house as soon as you came back, so I didn't want to bother you."

"I would have picked up," Rebecca assured her.

"And that's exactly why I didn't call you."

"How did we rectify the incident with Ann?"

"When I talked to Ann I assured her the cover would be corrected by the end of the next business day and Diane was ready to fire Vicky on the spot, but we decided it would be best to talk to you about it as well."

"I'm guessing you're the one who redid the whole cover," Rebecca responded.

"You know if anything around here is going to get done on time, I have to do it. I changed it back to the original cover but added a bit of my touch. Ann loved it and said she wants me to be in charge of her future book designs and promotional material from now on." Laura lit up.

"I'm so proud of you. Diane did an amazing job when she decided to bring you on the team. We need more young ladies with your skill around here," Rebecca said. "As far as Vicky, you can tell her to meet me in my office after lunch."

"I sure will," Laura smirked. "But enough about me and this place. How was the wedding? I can't believe I wasn't there, but instead playing mom to my niece."

"It was perfect. Beautiful scenery, quiet, and of course intimate in every way. I always thought I wanted to have a huge wedding, but this was exactly what I needed it to be."

"I can't wait to be someone's wife," Laura responded.

"Trust me, don't rush it. Wait until God places you and your soulmate together."

"How will I know if someone is my soulmate?" Laura asked.

"At first you won't. You'll be too blinded by what you believe is meant for you. Then out of nowhere something or someone will keep popping up in your life, even when you walk away. They will keep coming back around like a boomerang. Finally, something inside of your heart goes, *this is it!*"

"Is that how it went with Brandon?"

"It did and I hadn't even noticed." Rebecca blushed. "Sometimes we have to open our eyes a little wider to see what's been there all along."

* * *

Rebecca was standing at her desk, clearing away her milkshake and burger wrap when Vicky came knocking on her door. She hated that she had to be the one to reprimand Vicky, but someone had to do it or she was going to make them lose important clients.

"Hi Vicky, why don't you take a seat," Rebecca said, inviting her into the office. "I hope you enjoyed lunch."

"It was delicious," Vicky said sitting down nervously.

"Do you know why you are here?"

" I have an idea."

"Can you tell me why you felt it was okay to change around a book cover without getting anyone's permission first?" Rebecca asked leaning in.

Vicky had been with the publishing company for three years. Before Laura was hired, Vicky was the lead designer. A lot of clients had already been complaining about the cover designer not listening or fully comprehending what they were asking for, yet Diane insisted on keeping her around. Rebecca believed it was because they were friends and she didn't want any drama, but this was a business and she didn't need anyone working for them going rogue.

"Um," Vicky paused, "I thought she would want something that represented some of her older work, so I just went for it."

"Do you know why Ann insisted on coming to us for help?" Rebecca asked.

"Not exactly," Vicky said looking off to the side.

Rebecca got out of her chair and walked around to the other side of the desk, sitting on the edge. "It's because we promised to listen to her creativity, to communicate with her, and most importantly revamp her image. You would know that if you put your ego to the side and listened for once. This company has given you more chances than you deserve and today is your final warning. If you go out of your way to try to sabotage Laura or this company again you *will* be fired. Do you understand?" Rebecca asked.

"I understand Mrs. Bloom," Vicky said standing up to walk away.

"It's Mrs. Young now and before you go you need to remember why this company was created. We work best when we collaborate and motivate each other. We want to empower and make the women around us feel like their voices matter. This is a team and I want you to start working like you know that."

"I will do my best," Vicky said looking up at Rebecca.

"I really hope so."

22

A Session With Nasir

"Good afternoon Mr. Wright." Dr. Bell stood up to greet Nasir. "Glad I was able to get you into my schedule. Usually, I'm extremely booked but I am happy we were able to fit you in."

"Then this session must have been meant to be," he said shaking her hand.

"You can take a seat there." She gestured to the couch where she'd healed many of hearts and emotional scars. "So tell me about yourself and what brought you in?"

Nervously, Nasir began introducing himself like a kid on the first day of school. "I'm Nasir Wright from Richmond, California. I own a real estate company here in L.A. that's worth millions. I'm here today because I have anger issues and I'm not sure when they started. Either way, it's ruining all the relationships in my life. I'm a man with wealth, success, and no one to share it with." Nasir finished, wiping his sweaty palms on his pants. "That was awkward, " he said with his head down.

"No need to be nervous," Dr. Bell said. "I'm guessing this is your first time in a therapist's office?"

"Yeah...You know black people aren't usually into stuff like this, at least not where I'm from. On top of that, I never thought I'd be one of those people that needed to lay across some therapist's couch as I tell them about my fucked up life, but it's becoming apparent that I'm the problem when it comes to all the drama happening around me."

Sitting her notepad down on the desk, Dr. Bell sat straight up and focused all of her attention on Nasir. Most of the people that came into her office were apprehensive about speaking with her. In the black community, therapy wasn't something you were supposed to do. "Leave it up to God" or "Pray about it," are what most black men and women are told.

"I get it. Therapy is white people shit," Dr. Bell said in quotes, causing Nasir to let out a snicker, "and for people with real problems, but that isn't the case. Therapy can benefit everyone, no matter how big or small the issue. I've been in this position for 10 plus years and sometimes people just want a person to vent to, someone who knows nothing about them, holds no grudges, resentment, and or judgment towards them." Dr. Bell continued speaking, "I will never force you to talk about anything you aren't comfortable speaking on and if a day comes that you feel like therapy is not for you, that is alright too."

"I wouldn't even know where to begin," Nasir said relaxing on the white sofa. "I had a child with my first love, but from the moment she reappeared in my life shit has been in shambles, and skeletons from my closet started to fall all over the place. Some I prayed no one, especially her, would never have to find out about."

"How long have you two been together?"

"Well, right now we aren't together."

"Would you like to be?"

"Yes and no," he said as he's eyes drifted around. "Um, she's the reason I'm here so I guess in a way this is my attempt at being a better man for her."

"Is she the one who suggested you try therapy out?"

"Indirectly. She caught me trying to go through her phone and it pissed her off like really pissed her off. Then she told me I needed to get some help."

"And you must have agreed with her or you wouldn't be here, right?"

"Yeah, that's right. I spent most of our teen years trying to shield her from people that hurt and disappointed her, now in our adult years, I've turned into the man who brings her down and makes her sad. I don't want that for us or our son," Nasir answered truthfully.

Sitting with Dr. Bell was soothing. Nasir hadn't opened up to anyone like this in a long time. Brandon was his go-to person, something like his therapist and he no longer had him around. *I might can get used to this*, Nasir thought as he and Dr. Bell continued their conversation.

23

The Ladies

To celebrate Rebecca's first day back in the office, the ladies decided to meet up at a cute little bar for drinks. Nasir got off work early since he had a last-minute therapy session so he agreed to stay home with their son so Ashley could have a fun night out.

"Who are you going to hang out with again?" Nasir asked making sure not to sound aggressive or defensive. He noticed Ashley was going out a lot more than usual. She suddenly had this whole group of friends that he knew nothing about and Nasir was starting to think she had met someone new, which wouldn't have been too far-fetched being they weren't together. Yet and still he was feeling jealous.

"Truthfully," Ashley hesitated, "I'm going to have some drinks with Regina, Nikki, Monica... and Rebecca."

Silence filled the room at the sound of Rebecca's name. Nasir scratched at his ears because he had to be hearing things. *Did I hear what I thought I heard or am I just imagining it?* Picking up his son, who was now standing in front of him, he sat down on the couch with him and took two deep breaths.

"Are you sure that's a good idea, Ash?"

"Yes. We are on good terms and to be real with you...I consider us friends," she said walking over to Nasir and sitting down next to him. To Ashley's surprise, he was handling the situation better than she thought he would. No outburst, no trying to avoid the conversation, and no running to the liquor cabinet to take a shot. *I know one day in therapy didn't fix him that fast*, she thought as she waited for his response.

"Are you fine with me being friends with your ex?" She followed up when he didn't speak.

"If I were to say yes I'd be lying to you Ashley," Nasir paused and looked at her while holding onto their son for comfort, "but, I don't want to hold you back from building connections whether they be new people or those from the past. Just make sure she's being genuine. I'd hate for you to open up to her, just for her to turn around and stab you in the back."

"I can promise you her intentions are pure."

"So where does that leave me?"

"I'm not sure I know what you mean," Ashley said placing her hand on Nasir's knee.

"I don't see room for me in this picture. Because of her, I lost my best friend, my brother."

"For every action, there's a reaction and without that, he wouldn't be here." Ashley leaned in to kiss their son. "You will always be in the picture. People are going to come and go, but this family we decided to have together is here to stay."

"I should have just paid you for today's session. You sound like the therapist." Nasir smirked.

"Nope keep her. This is the most real and calmest I've seen you in quite some time," Ashley said. Standing up she leaned down and kissed Nasir on the forehead, "I won't be gone long."

"Have fun..."

* * *

"First day back and someone is already on the verge of being fired," Rebecca said picking up her glass.

"As long as it's not me." Nikki chuckled. "Please say it's not me."

The girls laughed watching Nikki fidget in her seat. She was literally on edge waiting for Rebecca to respond.

"Girl take a shot and relax. You are the last person we are thinking about getting rid of."

"Seriously babe. You practically made that place."

"She's not lying," Rebecca said. "Without the success of your books, Pretty & Bold would have never made it as far as it has, so trust me when I say you are in good hands. Matter of fact, let's all make a toast to my favorite author, Nikki Shay."

The ladies raised their glasses of wine and in unison shouted out, "To Nikki Shay."

"Ladies, you're making me blush."

"Don't blush too much," Monica joked.

"We are all happy in our relationships." Regina eyed Monica. "Don't get me wrong, Nikki is fine as fuck, but I prefer a nice juicy link."

"Okay, that's just nasty Gina," Ashley chimed in, "and for the record I'm single, but Nikki definitely scares me, so even if I were into lady parts I'd stay far away from hers."

"Oh my goodness," Nikki got out of her seat and walked towards Ashley, "I never apologized to you for that night at the club. I acted like such an animal." Nikki pulled Ashley in for a hug, squeezing her tight. "I'm so so sorry."

"At least you weren't the one who almost did a full dive over the table," Rebecca said covering her face.

"It's okay, you were just there defending your friend. I get it," she paused, "and Rebecca, yo ass scared me just as much as Nikki." She laughed. "I thought I was gonna have to fight and my scary ass was not ready for the heat coming my way."

"Whew, let's not rehash that mess." Regina shook her head. "I was ready to take my ass home."

"If I recall, that's the night you turned a frog into a prince," Monica added.

"Aww babe, is that the night Regina took your man?" Nikki giggled.

"Ha ha very funny," Monica replied.

"You know what, they can film a show based on our lives because this shit is interesting," Rebecca said.

"And one or both of y'all men could film it," Nikki added.

"And Monica can be the star," Ashley chimed in. "I saw you in the movie about the twin's life and my goodness."

"You watched that?" Monica asked in shock.

"Me and Nasir. As much static as I've had with those twins, I also spent a huge chunk of my life with them and their mother, so I had to see how it turned out. No one could have portrayed her as you did. Rebecca and Regina, she would have loved you guys."

"Oh my god, don't make us cry," Rebecca said.

"I'm just saying," Ashley responded. "By the way, I think our plan just might work," she said looking directly at Rebecca.

"What plan? And why are we not a part of it?" Monica asked.

"We are trying to reconnect Nasir with Brandon since I'm hanging around you all now. It'll make things less awkward," Ashley said to Monica.

"What makes you think that'll work?"

"Because he knows I'm here right now."

"With Rebecca," Monica emphasized.

"With ME," Rebecca said at the same time. "Was he upset? He didn't yell at you, did he? Because we can beat his ass." Rebecca was two glasses in and she was in defense mode. She caught Monica rolling her eyes from the corner of hers, but she wasn't going to play into her schoolyard jealousy. Unlike Monica, Rebecca wasn't one to hold grudges. It took too much of her energy.

"You are so sweet, Rebecca." Ashley laughed. "But surprisingly he was very calm. He did bring up Brandon and that immediately told me he regrets not trying to save their friendship."

"Did he go to the therapist I referred?"

"He had his first session today," Ashley answered Regina.

"Damn we just missed out on all the tea," Nikki said looking at the ladies and over at Monica who was now sipping her drink quietly.

"Sorry ladies, it was a spare-of-the-moment plan we came up with," Rebecca said. "We're planning a trip for all of us though and we want you guys to come. All ideas are welcome. We figured somewhere secluded so Brandon and Nasir can't run away from each other."

"How about Joshua Tree or Palm Springs?" Nikki suggested. "I've been dying to get away and it just might help move my manuscript along."

"I'm down."

"Me too!"

"Whichever is fine with me."

"Same, and I'll be bringing the kiddo along, so I'll let Kim know she can bring Ari. She loves being around Little Nasir."

"Well, enough talk about those guys. Let's drink up," Monica said.

"And eat," Ashley added. "I'm starving."

24

Brandon & Gary

"Bro, your wife got my lady leaving the house too much, and that damn Ashley tagging along too."

"It's not my fault my wife is easy to love. I'm sure they wish they were married to her as well."

"I'm still surprised she and Ashley are all buddy-buddy and shit. According to Regina, they are two peas in a pod. Practically drooling over each other." Gary started making kissing faces. "All the ladies want a piece of that ass."

"No matter how old you get, you still manage to be childish as fuck," Brandon said shaking his head. "Something about that catastrophic moment at the baby shower brought those two together and there's nothing I can say to Rebecca that will make her end that friendship, nor do I want her to."

"And why's that?"

"Because she should be able to build friendships with who-ever she wants. I don't own her and I'd never try. Her friendship with Ashley isn't going to hurt me. She's smart. If she feels some funny shit is happening she'll be quick to end things."

"Speaking of friendships," Gary said picking up his drink,

"did you watch her latest video?"

"Nah I been busy. What's it about? Her and Clyde?"

"Yeah, she brought that nigga up, but I think she was trying to hint at you and Nasir getting back cool."

"You think or you know?" Brandon asked.

"Alright, I know."

"And how do you know this?" Brandon asked, already knowing Rebecca wanted them to rekindle their friendship.

"Because I was watching with Regina and you know that intuition shit that women get? Well, yeah whatever that shit is hit me so I straight up asked Regina what's the deal."

"Just like that?" Brandon raised his eyebrows and laughed.

"Okay not exactly like that, but I did ask her if it was about you two and they have this plan to get y'all back on good terms."

"Didn't know we were on bad ones." Brandon got up and walked towards the fridge to grab a beer. Gary followed behind him and sat down at the table.

"Shit ain't good either and I don't understand why you acting like everything is."

"It is G. I got a beautiful new home, a new show, and the most incredible woman rocking my last name. Life is good with or without Nasir. It's not like I was the one who ended the friendship."

"You kind of were and even if you weren't you didn't try to save it either."

"Are you my brother or his?" Brandon asked, slamming the bottle down on the table, almost breaking it.

"You're my blood, I know that B, but both of y'all are my brothers and you guys let a woman get in between that."

"No, he let a woman get between that. Did you forget that damn sit-down we had at the Bar & Grill? Did you forget who warned him about Kim being at his baby shower? I still had his back. He let his feelings for Rebecca and his disrespectful mouth mess up our brotherhood."

"But bro—"

"Bro what?"

"What about forgiveness? Can't you forgive him?" Gary asked.

"The question is can he forgive me? I'm not the one tripping. He lost the girl and I married her. It might sound fucked up, but it is what it is."

"You're right," Gary responded, not wanting to piss his brother off any more than he already had. It made no sense for them to be arguing about a woman he married, but Brandon was wrong and he refused to take even a little accountability for the way things turned out.

25

The Home of the Mr. and Mrs.

After a full month of planning, the day had come for Brandon and Rebecca to share their home with their friends. No one had been over except for Monica and Clyde and they hadn't got to see the final results. Rebecca was expecting the catered food around 2 p.m. and Brandon was going to put some meat on the grill for everyone to enjoy.

Rebecca was excited to be hosting their friends for the first time as husband and wife, a big change from being Brandon's girlfriend. Her place in his life was set in stone and no one would be coming to take it, *ever*. She would fight for him if it came down to it, but lucky for her she knew she would never have to, Brandon wouldn't let it come to that.

"Surprised you aren't up working out." Brandon rolled over and wrapped his arms around her. He was used to her 5:00 a.m. routine, one thing she adopted from her relationship with Nasir.

Rebecca was sitting up in bed with a book in one hand and coffee in the other. "I didn't want to exhaust myself before company came."

"Do we have to entertain today?" Brandon asked, laying his head in her lap.

"I would love to stay in bed with you all day, but yes. I'm dying to show off the house my husband bought for me."

"Well, that's no fun," Brandon whined.

"And what would your idea of fun be?" Rebecca asked, placing her coffee down on the nightstand.

Sliding the covers back, Brandon maneuvered his head directly between Rebecca's thighs. She wasn't wearing any panties, just how Brandon liked it. Every night Rebecca wore a sexy little gown, providing him access to his treasure at all times. Adjusting himself comfortably, Brandon took his hands and placed her legs over his shoulders. Caressing her thighs, he began to massage her clit with his tongue. Brandon wanted to get her nice and moist before going all in. He enjoyed the taste of her and flicking his tongue against her clit was going to get her juices flowing.

Peaking up at his wife, he could see Rebecca was in ecstasy. Taking his fingers, he gently inserted them into Rebecca and went on the hunt for her spot. He knew he found it when her thighs took hold and she began grinding against him. Brandon proceeded to suck on her clit while playing with her insides. She was dripping wet and he couldn't wait to put his dick deep inside her. He wanted to watch the faces she made as he made love to her. The expressions she made never got old, only sexier.

"Come here," Rebecca moaned.

* * *

"Oooweee, this is nice and we haven't even gone inside yet," Nicole said staring out the window as she and Ashley approached the Young residence.

"Now this is the kind of area I imagined my family in," Ashley said pulling into the driveway, "not that damn glass house Nasir is so in love with."

"Are you nervous to meet everyone?"

"Not really, but I am interested in seeing if Brandon is going to be an ass or not."

"If you and Rebecca are as close as you appear to be, I'm sure he's going to be the perfect gentleman."

Ashley followed the signs that directed them toward parking. Brandon and Rebecca had cones lined up so each of their guests had their own parking space and could easily exit if need be. Rebecca hated when she would attend events and then get stuck waiting for someone to move their vehicle. As Ashley parked, Nicole noticed a car next to them with a man sitting inside. As he opened the door her mouth dropped.

"Are you okay?"

"How do I look?" Nicole asked turning towards Ashley and adjusting her boobs in her button-up dress.

"You look stunning."

"Do you know who that guy is?"

"I have no clue but I'm sure we'll find out soon. Let's make our way inside," Ashley said grabbing their housewarming gift from the backseat.

* * *

The guys sat in the backyard drinking beers and talking with Brandon, as he grilled steak and lobster. Once the sun began to set they would turn on the two fire pits located outside; one close to the pool and the other on the deck, which Rebecca liked to call her little circle of heaven based on the shape and white decor.

"I see the wife got you out here working," Nick joked.

"Right, she got all that fancy food in there but got you out here on the grill like an old black man." Clyde laughed.

"Aye, I decided to do this on my own, but I can keep all this good food for myself and y'all can eat on sushi and cucumber sandwiches or whatever that shit is all night," Brandon said checking the temperature of his steaks.

"I'm not complaining. I'm gon need about two of them things right there," Gary said drooling over the food.

"Of course, you do fat ass," Brandon said handing Gary a paper towel. "Did Rebecca give you guys a tour of the house?"

"She basically said here's the living room, here's the kitchen, and Brandon is that way," Nick replied.

"Yeah, she obviously wanted to speak to the ladies without us around because she kicked us to the curb and snatched all of them up," Clyde added. "She didn't even introduce me to that fine-ass woman that came in with Nasir's baby mama. I caught her eyeing the hell out of me before I came inside."

"That's my sister bro, and her name is Nicole."

"She's pretty as hell." Clyde smiled.

"Man, be cool. I don't want to hear all that."

"Is she single?"

"Yes," Gary responded immediately. "Want me to introduce you?"

"Seriously G." Nick shook his head.

"Yes please...if it's okay with the young man," Clyde said looking over at Nick for slight approval.

"I'm sure you aren't her type," Nick said hoping he could stop Clyde from pressing up on his sister.

"BRO!" Brandon turned around and laughed.

"I guess we'll just have to find out," Clyde smirked.

Once Rebecca finished showing the ladies around the house and Brandon finished grilling, everyone sat down at the table in the dining room. Rebecca had always dreamed of hosting a dinner with people she considered family. The only thing missing in her life was a few kids running around and she was praying that it would happen soon. For the most part, she'd kept her mind off getting pregnant, but being in a home like this with Brandon and hearing all of Ashley's stories about being a mother, she was 200 percent ready to experience it.

The sun would be setting soon and it was time to turn up. Rebecca had a fresh set of bathing suits in all the lady's sizes waiting in the spare bedrooms upstairs and Brandon had swim trucks for the guys.

"Are you guys ready to take this party outside," Rebecca shouted.

"Oh shit. This sounds like it's going to get wild," Clyde said.

"But not too wild, right?" Ashley asked hesitantly.

"I wouldn't mind," Nicole said winking at Clyde.

"Seriously Nicole." Nick shook his head.

"Let the girl live." Kim nudged him.

"We have swimwear upstairs for you all to change into. You will find your names on each. While you guys change I'm going to pour us up some shots and I have a game for us to play. Also, please don't be afraid to let the liquor flow. We have more than enough room for you all to stay the night or simply sober up before you leave," Rebecca said. "Once you're changed come meet us by the pool."

By the time everyone came back outside, Brandon and Rebecca had the music playing as they danced hand-in-hand.

"Aren't they adorable?" Regina said wrapping her arms around Gary.

"They cute or whatever, but they ain't got nothing on us."

"Hey love birds, we're back." Nikki smiled at them.

"Great let's take some shots and play a game," Rebecca said.

"What's this game we're going to be playing?" Kim asked.

"It's going to be a fun yet raunchy game. A way to get to know each other better. I know a lot of us have been friends for a long time and then of course we have siblings in the house, but everyone has a few secrets to tell." Rebecca smirked.

"This is going to be super fun or get real messy." Ashley looked around.

"My sister isn't here so I'm sure we'll be okay," Regina added, causing everyone to laugh. All those who knew Shantel knew she was the messiest person around. She lived for the drama.

"Am I missing something?" Kim asked.

"Right, fill us in," Clyde added.

"Shantel is Regina's messy half-sister. She pretty much hates every last one of us, yet somehow always found her way into one of our group outings. I'm pretty sure if she knew we were having a party here, she'd find a way to crash," Rebecca answered. "Oh, and let me add that she also dated my husband for a while."

"And tried to seduce his brother shortly after," Regina said grabbing hold of Gary as if her sister would come around the corner any second.

"That's some fucked up shit. If that was my sister—"

"Be happy it isn't," Regina said cutting Kim off. "Enough about her though. Let's drink up and enjoy the rest of the night,"

"Cheers to that!" Everyone raised their shot glasses.

26

Monica

Monica watched from the patio couch as everyone drank and laughed, including her girlfriend. For the first time in a long time, she felt like she wasn't a part of the group. In all honesty, she was jealous of how much fun everyone was able to have without her. Monica let Nikki enjoy herself for a while longer and then she swept her away without a goodbye to the others.

While in the car Nikki noticed Monica wasn't in the best mood, but she didn't want to get into it with her about why they were leaving when the fun was just beginning. Monica barely drank or interacted with anyone and although Nikki noticed it she refused to acknowledge it at the moment. There was no point in ruining a good time. Monica was typically the life of the party; friendly, always making jokes and dancing. She loved to entertain, but tonight it was different.

Once they got on the road Nikki finally spoke up. "Babe, are you sure you're alright?"

"I'm good, why?"

"You just seemed like you were in a rush to get out of there.

Thought something might be wrong."

"I'm fine. Just a little tired and want to be home in our bed. Nothing more than that," Monica lied.

"You know Rebecca had a room for us. You could have laid down."

"Did you not hear me say I want to be in my bed?"

Nikki could sense the attitude, but she was too drunk to push the issue. The only outcome would be a heated argument and in the state, she was in, no good would come from that. Leaning her chair back, she closed her eyes and drifted off to sleep. Monica cracked the window for her slightly, so she wouldn't start to feel sick.

I feel like I'm losing my best friend, Monica thought to herself as she navigated through the playlist on her phone. These days, she and Rebecca barely talked to each other and it seemed like Ashley and Regina knew more about what was happening in her life than she did. From secret meetups to plans to reunite her ex-boyfriend with her new husband. It was weird. On top of that, Rebecca hadn't even asked her how filming was going or anything that related to her career.

As Monica dived deep into her thoughts the Bluetooth on her car announced there was a new message on her phone. Not wanting to wake Nikki, she decided to pull over for a second to read the message. She was desperate to know what it said. Monica was surprised Rebecca even noticed she left.

Rebecca: *Please please let me know when you make it home. I wish you would have stayed. Now that the house is together let's have a sleepover. We can binge Gossip Girl or rewatch Desperate Housewives. I love you* *so much!*

"I guess she hasn't forgotten about me completely," Monica mumbled before making her way back on the road.

"Why would she? That's gonna be your girl for life," Nikki managed to say before falling back to sleep.

27

Nasir and Ashley

"I was wondering when you'd make it back home."

"Did you miss me?"

"Not really—"

"Rude," Ashley said throwing her jacket at him.

Catching it he laughed and said, "You didn't even let me finish."

"If you're not going to tell me you miss me, I don't want to hear it," she responded with her hands over her ears.

Nasir let Ashley stand in the middle of the floor waiting to get her way. He wanted her mind to wonder. *Did he miss her? Did he not?* It had been a while since he said those words, but he did. Her being away from home more than he was used to, made it clear to him, especially after tonight. He would have preferred she be home with him or to at least be out having a good time with her.

"I guess not," she said making her way toward the room with her hands still over her ears.

"I miss you."

"Huh, I can't hear you," Ashley stopped in her tracks, "I

think I'm going deaf."

Standing up, Nasir walked over to Ashley and removed her hands from her ears. "I said that I, Nasir Wright, missed the hell out of you while you were gone. You know how deathly silent it gets in here once the little guy closes his eyes for the night."

Making a sad face and poking out her lips, Ashley whined, "So you only missed me because it was too quiet?"

"No that's not the only reason. You're my best friend."

"And you're mine. I thought I'd at least make it back to put him to bed and spend some time with you."

"Not smelling like that." Nasir plugged his nose. "Did Nicole drive you home?"

"Don't be mad," Ashley grabbed Nasir's hands, "I drove myself."

"Ash, you know I don't like that shit. What if something happened? My heart would stop and me and Little Nasir's world would come crashing down."

"I know I'm sorry. Rebecca offered me a room, but I couldn't leave you two home alone for the whole night," Ashley paused and stepped closer to him, "and I also missed you."

Being in a house full of couples madly in love with each other had Ashley in her feelings. She wondered if she and Nasir would ever make it back to that place. She wanted to so badly, but every time they got close, something interfered. Nicole even managed to make a connection while they were out. Within two hours Nicole and Clyde were stuck to each other like glue. Ashley couldn't remember the last time she had seen her sister laugh that hard. Clyde looked slightly goofy, but Ashley had to admit that he was pretty damn handsome. Nick was disgusted at the display of affection they were showing to one another.

Instead of forcing her to come home, she took her chances and headed out so she could be with her own little family. Nasir might not have currently been her man, but he was the father of her son and the love of her life. She couldn't fathom being anywhere else.

"I thought you hated me."

"I could never hate you. Be annoyed with you? Absolutely." She placed her hand on his chest, "I'm going to go take a shower." Ashley turned around and started walking towards the room, "Would you like to join? I could use some help."

Do I join her or do I keep my ass on my side of the house? Nasir didn't know what his next move should be so he stood there frozen. He and Ashley hadn't been intimate since their son was born and the sexual tension was thick. If he was going to go in there and cross the line of friendship they created, there would be no going back this time.

Ashley watched him as his mind played through every scenario possible. "I promise it's not the liquor talking," she said as she began undressing. "I will always choose you."

Taking off his shirt, Nasir walked towards Ashley, "You got me...Always."

28

The Guys

T he trip planned by the women was finally set in stone. Separately they talked to their men and refused to let up until everyone agreed to go. Brandon had no choice but to say yes to his wife. Nasir took some convincing but eventually said yes to staying in Ashley's good graces. After talking to his therapist he came to realize it was a great step in the direction of finding the closure he needed and possibly rekindling old friendships. Knowing Ashley and their son would be there also eased his mind. Kim also agreed to attend their little getaway and it was the only way to convince Nick to go as well. She knew he missed spending time with his sisters and nephew and this would be the perfect space for that. Gary on the other hand was always going to be a yes, but he refused to be on a trip with a bunch of guys who couldn't get out their feelings.

Gary sent out a group text to the guys telling them it was mandatory to meet him at the Boxing Gym. Gary knew the gym owner and he owed Gary a favor, so he allowed them private access to the gym for a day. If Nasir, Nick, and Brandon didn't want to talk out their problems he was going to make them box it out instead. He invited Clyde along for the hell of it. He wanted to see if he could truly hang with the big boys. Gary wasn't sure why Brandon thought it was a good idea to bring him back around, but he wasn't really feeling him. He never understood how a male and female could be best friends and not have any feelings involved. Brandon and Rebecca were practically best friends and they ended up married.

"Look at that," Gary smirked as each of the guys entered the gym one by one. "Right on time." Gary was standing in the middle of the gym facing the entrance with his arms folded over.

"Happy to be here." Clyde grinned.

"Yeah, we'll see how you feel about it once this is all over," Gary snapped.

"Don't mind him," Brandon said patting Clyde on the back of the shoulder. "He can be a little intense at times."

"I can see that."

"Wassup bro? Why you got all of us here early as hell?" Nick questioned Gary.

"I'm always down for a workout, but this ain't that," Nasir said looking at Gary and then back at the guys, focusing most of his attention on Brandon.

"We about to take this back to those Richmond days," Gary said walking towards the ring, gesturing the guys to follow him. "Remember how Mama used to make us go out in them streets whenever we found ourselves at odds?"

"How could I forget?" Nasir shook his head but had a slight smile on his face.

"Yeah I used to beat the brakes off you," Brandon responded.

"Things change," Nasir said turning towards Brandon.

"Anyways," Gary interrupted, "no matter how angry we were, after getting out all that aggression we were back good with one another. Since everyone here seems to have a problem—"

"Only one with a problem is that nigga over there." Nick pointed at Nasir.

"Since everyone seems to have a problem with that nigga over there, we about to get in this ring and fix it before we go on this damn vacation."

"Um...why am I here?" Clyde asked with his hand raised in the air.

"Cause nigga, I just don't trust you. You hurt my sister-in-law's feelings now you back in the picture as if you haven't been some non-existent ass nigga. You got secrets and if I gotta beat 'em out of you on my brother and his wife's behalf I will."

"I'd much rather you not," Clyde said looking Gary up and down. He wanted no part in what these dudes were about to get into. Besides Nick, he knew the other three were star football players and they kept themselves in excellent shape. Clyde preferred to leave the boxing gym with his face intact. That was the one thing he had going for himself, besides his goofy personality.

"Then reveal your secret and you're free to go—"

"Or stay," Brandon added.

"Y'all still might want to fight me after this."

"Just spit it out already man. I'm sure it's not worse than finding out your sister's baby daddy dated and beat up your current girlfriend," Nick blurted out.

The awkward silence was broken by the sound of Nasir hitting a punching bag. It sounded like it was going to burst.

"You sure you wanna fight him?" Gary said looking over at his brother.

"I will since he wanna hit somebody so bad," Nick said walking towards the ring. "I'm sure it's been a while...or has it?"

"Man, fuck all y'all," Nasir said hitting the bag again. "Nick, what happened with Kim was the biggest mistake of my life but if you need to fight me to feel better about it go ahead. And Brandon, you...you took my bitch and said fuck me completely."

Stepping up to Nasir, Brandon looked him dead in the eyes before punching him in the jaw, causing Nasir to stumble backward. "I told you about using that bitch word when it comes to my wife. The only person acting like a bitch around here is you. This shit could have been resolved over a year ago, but here you are still crying about what you lost."

Gary stepped between the two of them to make sure Brandon didn't double back on Nasir. "Aye, we not about to do it like this. Grab the gloves and get in the ring. Handle it the right way."

"That was a bitch ass move B," Nasir said wiping the blood from his mouth.

"You kinda deserved it," Clyde said shaking his head. "Rebecca is the last person you should refer to as a bitch and she wasn't yours to own."

"Fuck you, Clyde. Yo ass probably wanted her too," Nasir responded.

"You got me there. You wanted to know my secret," Clyde said looking toward Gary and the rest of the guys. "I was falling in love with Rebecca. That's why I disappeared from her. For my good. Sure I hurt her, but I was hurting more so I had to take a break from that friendship."

"You know what? I respect that," Gary responded. "How you feel about that brother?"

"I already knew. All those years spent with her and the stories she told me. There was no doubt that you were in love with her. It was only natural and I told her that, but you're her best friend and I feel like I've been around you enough to know you won't cross that line. Right?"

"Hundred percent correct," Clyde responded. "Plus I think I found my wife. That sister of yours is a fucking Goddess," he said with a look of satisfaction.

"And you better not fucking forget it." Nick raised his fist.

"Welp, one issue resolved. Now back to you two. Are you going to fight or what?" Gary asked.

"He just gonna get his ass beat and that's it. Nasir is not ready to forgive me for finding my person," Brandon said stepping into the ring.

Brandon and Nasir fought a full twelve rounds. He was giving Brandon a run for his money, but the longer they fought, Gary could see the hurt and rage draining from him. Brandon took a step back as Nasir swung at him and he countered with an uppercut, knocking Nasir flat on his back. This was more than a fight about a woman, this was years of pent-up aggression. Nasir was jealous of Brandon for being able to get whatever he wanted and Brandon was tired of always covering Nasir's tracks; making sure he remained down the right one. Everyone leaned on Brandon and never offered him a shoulder. The moment he found some happiness, the one person he constantly rode for wasn't there to support him. Without saying a word, Brandon exited the gym, leaving everyone to wonder if they were in a better or worse position.

"Should I go after him?" Clyde asked Gary.

"No, he'll be fine. He just needs to take some time to cool off and reflect."

Nasir lay on the floor exhausted and as much as Nick wanted to go at him next, he didn't think Nasir could handle it. Stepping into the boxing ring, Nick approached Nasir, handing him a wet towel and a hand.

"Do you even know why Ashley broke up with you back then?" Nick asked Nas as he helped him off the mate.

"Yes, but not until we reconnected. Before that I had no clue what happened to all of you back then," Nasir answered. "In my naive mind, I thought she no longer needed me to be her saving grace. I felt abandoned."

"Yet you were still aware of all the shit we had to put up with back in Richmond before you went off to be a college boy." Nick reminded him. "So instead of trying to get over my sister you decided to make someone else a victim because you couldn't handle rejection. Is that what you're trying to tell me?".

"That truly wasn't my intention. Kim didn't deserve what happened to her that night and to be honest, I can barely remember what I did. All I know is I hurt her and after that, I never saw her again. At least not until that night at the Bar & Grill. You have to believe me when I say I'm not that person and I would never do a thing like that again." Nasir's eyes were starting to water. "How can I make this right? I have to make it right. We supposed to be a family. I'm tired of fighting my brothers." Nasir was on his knees begging for Nick's forgiveness. "What do I need to do?"

"Man get up," Nick said pulling at his shoulders. He could feel Nasir's remorse and see the regret on his face through all the blood. "The only way to make this right is to give Kim an apology."

"I will," Nasir said standing up.

"And don't stop apologizing no matter how long it takes for

her to forgive you. She needs closure more than any of us and I believe you're the only person that can provide it."

"If I have to apologize up until the day y'all lay me to rest, I promise you I will." Nasir reached his arms out towards Nick, hoping he would welcome his attempt at a hug.

"You know you wanna hug that nigga. Just do it," Gary said pushing Nick into Nasir's arms.

29

Brandon & Rebecca

"I HATE THIS SHIT!"

Brandon banged his hands against the steering wheel and screamed. His adrenaline was still pumping and he wanted to go in the gym and take it out on Nasir some more. Before he knew it he felt his eyes swell up. He thought it was from the hits he took to the face, but then he felt a stream of water rolling down his cheeks. Brandon was crying. It took this moment for him to realize he'd been avoiding mourning his lost connection with his best friend.

"Babe, what's wrong?"

Brandon managed to facetime Rebecca, but he didn't know what to say to her. All he knew was he was hurting and he needed to see her.

"Come home, please."

Without a word, he blew her a kiss and hung up the phone. Brandon sped all the way home and once he got there he busted through the door like the police and rushed to Rebecca's side. She was standing in the middle of the living room waiting for him to arrive. They shared each other's location and she tracked him all the way home. Brandon took hold of Rebecca and cried. This was the first time she saw him break down like this. He cried on their wedding day, but those were tears of joy. What she was seeing now was a man broken.

"Babe, talk to me," she said rubbing his head. "I can't fix it if you don't say anything."

"I miss my brother."

Rebecca knew he wasn't talking about Gary, they saw each other faithfully. He was speaking of his childhood best friend; the one person he didn't need to share blood with to call family, the one person he could depend on no matter what, the person he shared his triumphs with and so much more. Brandon and Nasir had a bond that she would never be able to understand. They were both missing out on so much in each other's lives and it was all because she came into the picture. If only Brandon had approached her that night, maybe all of this could have been avoided.

"I can't see you like this," Rebecca said doing her best to get Brandon off the floor. His hurt was tearing her apart and she hated being the cause of it.

"I let your brother do it his way, now we are going to do it mine. Go get yourself cleaned up. I'm fixing this shit *today*." Rebecca kissed Brandon and grabbed her phone.

* * *

Brandon took an ice-cold bath and then a hot shower. Once he calmed down, all he felt was pain. *That nigga beat my ass.* Brandon swallowed two pain pills. Throwing on sweatpants and a matching crewneck, Brandon brushed his waves to perfection and headed down the stairs.

"Wifey, I feel so much—" Brandon stopped speaking when he spotted Nasir and Ashley sitting in the family room with Rebecca. She had two glasses full of whiskey seating on the table, one directly in front of Nasir. The last place he expected to see him was sitting in his living room, in front of his wife. He felt ambushed. "What is this?"

"I told you I was going to handle this my way," Rebecca said standing up. "Come sit down."

"I'm glad to see Nasir isn't the only one looking a mess." Ashley snickered in an attempt to cut the tension.

Brandon glanced over at them and noticed they were sitting hand-in-hand. "You two back together?"

"We are," Nasir answered for her.

Another moment I missed out on, but at least he won't be coming for my woman again.

"Seems like therapy is working for you," Rebecca said pulling Brandon down next to her. "I'm not stalking you by the way," Rebecca emphasized as Nasir looked at her awkwardly. "My girl right here has become something like my right hand. We tell each other almost everything and that's why we need the two of you to get your shit together. How can we be the best of friends when our men aren't even speaking?"

"Straight to the point." Ashley winked at Rebecca. "The disconnect between you two all started because of us and now we're here to put everything back in order."

"This has nothing to do with the two of you," Nasir snapped.

"Lower your voice," Brandon snapped back.

"Both of you shut the fuck up and listen."

"Ooh, Becca. I love this side of you," Ashley said proudly.

"Is this a joke to you guys?" Nasir looked at both of them.

"I honestly wish it were, but it's not. Ashley is right. This started with us. You cheated on me with her and I ended up marrying your best friend. I understand why you did it and it hurt at the moment, but I found who was truly meant for me."

Curious, Nasir asked, "What is it you understand?"

"That you never got over Ashley and you looked for her in every woman you came across. Kim could pass for her twin if she were slightly taller and cut her hair off. Then there's me—"

"You look nothing like Ashley," Brandon interjected.

"But we have very similar personalities and characteristics."

Brandon couldn't deny that. She and Ashley were strong, independent, career-driven women who cared deeply about their loved ones and could adapt to any environment they were in and no matter where they went people gravitated toward them. The only thing they didn't share was the trauma Ashley had to endure.

"Okay, say that is true, what does that have to do with him dating you? That's completely against bro code." Nasir picked up his drink and took it back. The bottle was sitting on the table in front of them so Ashley picked it up and poured him another. Today he needed one, but she was impressed with how calm both of the guys were handling things. *Gary's idea to have them fight it out must not have been so bad after all.*

"You have to stop blaming Brandon. He would have looked in the opposite direction and probably kept dating that bitch Shantel if I hadn't opened the door for him to walk through."

Once again everyone managed to break the tension by sharing a laugh about Shantel. Brandon's life would have been hell and they all knew it.

"I'm sorry we hurt you, Nasir," Rebecca continued, "but just like you couldn't ignore your feelings for Ashley, I couldn't ignore mine for Brandon. This man right here," Rebecca said gently grabbing Brandon by the chin, "was my last chance at finding true happiness. I couldn't pass that up and I hope you understand that. So please don't be mad at him, be mad at me. As much as he acts like he's fine without you in his life, trust me when I say he needs you more than ever."

"And Nasir needs you, Brandon. He has no fucking friends, like none." Ashley chuckled, but she was serious. "And don't say he has Gary because that man is not good when it comes to anything slightly serious."

"Thanks for making me sound like a loser." Nasir squinted his eyes at Ashley.

Brandon wanted to laugh because he knew how terrible Gary was when it came to listening to anyone's problems other than his. That was always Brandon's job; he could have fun, but he also knew when to be serious and empathetic.

"I didn't like it, but I've been seeing a therapist as you know and I'm accepting things for what they are. You two have always been close, but you guys could have broken it to me easy," he directed his comments towards Brandon, "but instead I had to see you two walk hand-in-hand into a restaurant together."

"Don't forget the part where you were tonguing down Ashley," Brandon side-eyed Nasir, "but you are right, as your friend, no as your brother, I should have been a man and spoke up. I'm sorry for that."

"Um, can we leave my name out of this?" Ashley asked sarcastically.

"Oh, hell no." Rebecca laughed. "I remember that nasty ass kiss. You're one hundred percent in it."

"Who would have thought?"

"Crazy right," Brandon said knowing he and Nasir were thinking the same thing. Rebecca and Ashley were truly friends and they were pretty sure nothing would get between them.

"So, can we celebrate? Has this decade-long relationship been fixed?" Ashley asked standing up.

"Now you know it's been well over a decade, but Nasir—"

"You don't even have to ask," Nasir stood up and moved closer to Brandon, "I forgive you and I'm sorry for being an ass."

Nasir didn't give Brandon a chance to stand up. He snatched him off the couch and wrapped him in a bear hug. The stress of the world washed away the second he wrapped his arms around Brandon. Pushing him off, Brandon leaned back and grunted, "Damn, nigga are you not in the same physical pain I am?"

"I told you we weren't kids no more," Nasir said getting into a boxing stance.

"Nope, no more. I don't want to fight your strong ass ever again."

"Oh, how things change." Ashley laughed. "Back in the day, Brandon used to whoop Nasir and Gary's ass. He wanted to prove to his mom he was the leader of the pack so bad."

"I hope our kids get to grow up the same." Rebecca placed her hand on her stomach and smiled.

"Rebecca..." Ashley paused and stared at her as if her eyes worked like her own personal sonogram machine. "Are you trying to tell us something?"

Rebecca was extremely consumed with work and being a wife, that she failed to realize she missed not one, but two periods. They were already pretty irregular, but more so when she was stressed. Married life was going well, but her job was becoming overwhelming due to the lack of respect her employees had for her. Rebecca had always been a hard worker, even before becoming part owner of the publication and she refused for her team to continue to slack off and make stupid mistakes. She was now liable for those and she wasn't going to hesitate to get rid of who she needed and the girls hated her for it. There was no more nice Rebecca when it came to the business and Diane backed her on that.

Over the past few weeks, she had become more exhausted than usual. Her days were filled with going over manuscripts, overseeing designs, and meetings, so she thought it was just her body adjusting. That was until the weird cravings for food she didn't even enjoy and cramping kicked in. That's when she decided to check her period tracker and in bold it said, "*take a pregnancy test*." Scared of the outcome, she avoided it for a few days and the spotting started. *My period is finally here*, she thought to herself but it stopped a day later. Worry took over Rebecca, which lead her to schedule an appointment with her doctor, and in that office, she confirmed she was pregnant. She planned to surprise Brandon with dinner and a basket full of gifts, but the drama in their friend group was overshadowing her plans.

As happy as Rebecca was to be pregnant she was terrified she'd leave Brandon disappointed in the end. *What if I lose this baby like I lost the last? It could turn out to be the end of my marriage. After all, it ended my first engagement.*

"Just that you guys better be at the first birthday party?"

"Are you pregnant?" Ashley jumped up and down excitedly. "Of course you're pregnant."

Both Nasir and Brandon looked at each other eyes wide. For so long Rebecca thought she couldn't have a baby and she contemplated ending her relationship with Brandon because of it. Even after confirming everything was fine with her eggs and Brandon's sperm, never once did she end up pregnant and there was never a moment Brandon pulled out.

"She's Pregnant!" they both said together.

Brandon automatically forgot about everything that happened to them before this. All the pain Brandon had been feeling vanished. The day had started so low but was ending on a high note. His wife was carrying his legacy and he was going to cater to her as much as he could. Becoming a father meant everything to him and now it was happening.

"I'm pregnant," she confirmed. "I wish I didn't have to tell you with your face all ugly though. Thanks a lot, Nas." She folded her arms over.

"You better not let Monica find out you told us first," Nasir put his hands in the air, "or your face is going to match your husband's."

"She looks like she hits hard too and I don't think she likes me very much, so I won't be saying a word." Ashley put her thumb and index finger together and pretended to zip her mouth shut.

Rebecca laughed, but she knew Nasir was right. Monica would be pissed if she knew the ex and the woman he cheated on her with found out before she did. She would call her over for the sleepover and binge session she promised. That would be the perfect moment to tell her.

"This will be our little secret for now. Should we cross our hearts?" Rebecca asked

"And hope to die," Ashley continued.

"Stick a needle in your eye," they both yelled out like school girls.

30

Rebecca & Monica

"Is Nikki fine with me taking you for the night? I know she can't stand being alone," Rebecca said plopping down on the bed next to Monica. They wore matching pajamas with sheep on them and pink fuzzy socks.

"She'll be fine. She said she wanted to work on a few of those edits you sent to her," Monica said, digging her hand into the popcorn bowl. "She's invested in this new erotic thriller genre she's exploring and it's had her stuck on the laptop for hours."

"I don't know why that woman is nervous. The plot twists in that book are award-winning excellence okay, but don't tell her I said that. I want to see how this second draft turns out." Rebecca snickered.

Monica nodded in agreement. "So what do you have me watching tonight?"

"I wanted us to watch Gossip Girl, but I know our old asses will be asleep before we get through two episodes so I figured we just scroll through Netflix and see what we can find."

"I'm not old yet. I'm down to binge a show. If we don't finish that just means you have to set up weekly BFF dates with me to finish and I don't have a problem with that. We haven't binged a good show since The Vampire Diaries."

"And to think...you used to give me hell about it," Rebecca said smiling. Closing Netflix, she headed over to HBO Max to put on Gossip Girl.

"Shall, I go grab the wine?" Monica asked getting out the bed, but Rebecca grabbed her hand to stop her.

"I can't drink."

"Why not?"

"What reason would there be for a wino like me not to have a glass or two?" Rebecca adjusted herself on the bed, waiting for her best friend to register what she was telling her.

"Um, because you drink too much," Monica said slipping her hand from Rebecca's grip so she could go grab a bottle.

"Guess again silly and think harder this time."

Stumped, Monica stood still with one knee on the bed thinking of all the reasons one wouldn't drink. To Rebecca the answer was clear, but Monica seemed lost. As Rebecca was about to blurt out the words, Monica started to cry.

"O-oh-my-god, we're having a baby." Walking around to Rebecca's side of the bed she pulled her in close and held onto her. "I knew you'd get to be a mom one day. I knew it."

Rebecca took a tissue from the box on the nightstand and wiped the tears from Monica's face. "I wanted to ask you a question."

"Anything."

"Would you do me the honor of being our baby's fairy godmother?"

"Position accepted. I'll be the best fucking godmother there ever was. And to think I thought I was losing you to the new girl."

"Ashley?" Rebecca smirked. "You've got to admit...she's refreshing."

Monica rolled her eyes, still not all the way onboard the Ashley train. "She's a man thief."

Rebecca burst into laughter. She couldn't believe how immature Monica was being. She hated for Rebecca to be close to anyone that wasn't her. If Nikki wasn't her girlfriend, she'd be throwing shady remarks her way as well. For the longest it was just Monica and Rebecca; no one else to lean on and laugh with. Now, Rebecca had this new circle of friends she was building strong connections with. Everyone wanted a piece of her and Monica just wasn't ready to share.

"And I'm a best friend fucker." Rebecca snorted. "I've sensed the tension. I know you've been a little jealous, but I need you to know that no one will ever take your place. Not in this lifetime or the next. Yes, I'm building a new friendship, but you, you're my person, my soulmate, and I love you with everything in me. I'm sorry I haven't been checking on you like I usually do. I just got so caught up in trying to fix Nasir and Brandon."

Raising an eyebrow Monica asked, "How's that going?"

"Sickening," Rebecca made a gagging sound.

"So they still hate each other?"

"The opposite. I caught them on facetime the other day and they both were cheesing from ear to ear. I know I said I wanted them to fix their friendship, but it's like they're newly married."

"At least that means we don't have to worry about anyone fighting when we head out for this trip next week," Monica said as she crawled over Rebecca to get back to her side of the bed.

"I'm surprised Clyde didn't tell you." Rebecca adjusted herself to face Monica. "When everyone agreed to the trip Gary had them on some fight club shit. My husband came home crying and looking a got damn mess."

"Clyde hasn't told me a damn thing, except for the fact that he was falling in love with you. Did you know?

"I had my suspicions. Brandon told me it's practically impossible for men and women to be friends without catching some kind of feelings."

"That's evident," Monica said looking at the ring on her friend's finger. It was blinding.

"Anyways," Rebecca laughed, "I just wish he would have said something instead of ghosting me."

"Would that have changed anything?" Monica asked out of curiosity.

"Hmm, I'm not sure." Rebecca turn on her back and looked towards the ceiling. "I used to think that maybe one day we'd get married and have kids, but then he disappeared. It probably wouldn't have worked. He's kind of a jerk."

"That I can agree on. I know you had other plans for your life and you were starting to think none of this would happen for you, but look at you now. You're a boss, a wife with a husband a lot of women dream of, and now a bun in the oven. Those other men were not meant for you and the man up there knew that." Monica leaned over to embrace Rebecca. "I can't wait to find out what we are having." Monica placed her hand on Rebecca's stomach, "I hope it's a little you."

"Me too!"

31

Day 1

The group agreed on renting two houses in Yucca Valley just up the road from each other. They hadn't realized how big of a group they were when they came together since they had gotten used to doing everything in smaller groups. Each day they would switch off who would host lunch and dinner. Since Ashley, Nasir, Kim, and Nick had children they decided to stay together along with Gary and Regina. The rest of the clan would be in the other house up the road.

"I cannot believe you two got all of us out here. It's hot, but it's just the solitude I need from the city," Regina said pulling Rebecca and Ashley into a hug, "and that pool...can't wait to jump in."

"Woman you act like you've been overwhelmed by the job you no longer have," Gary said rolling past with their luggage.

Kicking her feet towards him Regina yelled out, "You're lucky there are children around or I'd—"

"Or you'd what? Sit me down with another therapist?" He smirked and walked into their home for the weekend.

"Seriously, how do you put up with him?" Ashley rubbed

Regina's back. "He's always been so ugh."

"Therapy," she replied and they all laughed. "Let's go check out the inside."

"This is beautiful," Rebecca said walking into the black desert home, which was surrounded by white brick walls that blocked off any intruders but still provided a beautiful view of the sandy brown desert surrounding them. "I wonder what our place looks like in person. The pictures were beautiful, but these home renters know how to create an illusion."

"You'll find out shortly," Ashley said.

The house was huge and each couple's bedroom had either a King or Queen sized bed. The couples with the children took the two rooms with King beds and ample space to move around. There was a pool and Jacuzzi in the beautiful backyard, which had an outdoor dining area and fire pit.

"Did anyone bring bug spray?" Nasir yelled out, swatting his hands in the air and then hitting his arm. "These bugs are already trying to take me out."

"I have some right here," Kim said digging into her bag and handing Nasir the bottle. "I see you still can't stand insects."

"Yeah, I should have thought twice about agreeing to come to this place. There's no telling what I'm going to wake up to," he said twitching and scratching at his skin. "They're *everywhere*."

"You're a big man. You'll be alright."

"Yeah, you'll be a-okay Uncle Nas." Ari gave him a thumbs up.

"Thank you, Princess." He bent down to hug her.

"I'm going to go play with my little cousin now," she said running off.

Kim and Nasir's relationship was still pretty shaky, but at least she could finally stomach being in the same room as him.

She didn't find herself in a corner counting to ten or speaking affirmations to calm her anxiety whenever she looked at him. Nasir had spent weeks apologizing to Kim; for babysitting Ari constantly, treating them to lunch, dinner, and movies. He was sticking to his word and doing what he could for her forgiveness. Kim couldn't even remember spending that much time with him in the short time they dated. Quite frankly, she was getting overwhelmed with the apologies and begged him to stop. Seeing how he interacted with Ari eased her mind. Kim knew that he had a genuine heart and though he hurt her in the past, she knew it wouldn't happen a second time.

Everything was coming together perfectly. Nick was back spending time with his sister and nephew, Kim started going to Sunday dinners at Nasir's house, and Ari and Little Nasir were inseparable. If she was allowed, she'd see him every day. Most importantly, Ashley was back to herself; no longer stressing over her family being on bad terms or walking around on eggshells around Nasir.

* * *

"I could see the Flintstones living here," Brandon said eyeing the exterior of the house before making his way inside. The modern design gave off Bedrock mixed with Lego vibes. If everyone wanted, they could grab sleeping bags and sleep on top of the house since the roof was completely flat. Brandon was already thinking of ways he and Rebecca could get up there to make love, but with her being pregnant she probably wouldn't go for it.

"Really?" Monica said looking at Brandon. "Only you."

"Come on, tell me you don't see it. If the Flintstones came

up on millions of dollars and decided to renovate their home *this*," Brandon opened his arms wide, "would be it."

"I can see it," Nikki said strolling past them into the house.

"Says the director and writer. Of course, you guys see it," Monica said running after Nikki. "Let's go pick a room."

"The master is me and the wife's so don't even try it," Brandon blurted out. Knowing Monica she would try to get the best room in the house. Rebecca had stopped at the other house to make sure everyone settled in fine, because she's just that nice, and he did not want to get cussed out when she got back. "I'm serious," he yelled to her just in case she didn't hear the first time.

"Thanks for letting us stay with you guys." Nicole was now next to Brandon.

"Of course. I know you and Clyde are newly dating and being in a house with kids and your siblings would have killed the mood."

"You get it." She winked and walked inside with Clyde following closely behind.

Once inside, Brandon sat down their bags. Monica indeed did not take the master, but he knew Nikki would have loved it. Sitting off to the side was a bookshelf-desk combination, that he was positive she would be using to work on her book. The glass sliding door led right to the backyard, which had a bow-tied shape swimming pool in clear view. One side of the bow was a Jacuzzi and the other was the swimming pool. Each room had a door that led outside, but the master room had the best view. There was enough space back there for everyone to sit and relax while keeping a distance. Brandon was extremely excited about the grill. The garage was also converted into a room with a pool table and a pullout sofa. The guys would be spending free time in there for sure.

"What's on the agenda for today?" Clyde asked walking into the backyard already in his swim trunks.

"You just couldn't wait could you?"

"We are on vacation aren't we?" He jumped in before Brandon could answer.

* * *

The guys came together for what typically used to be a night out at the Bar & Grill. It was a tradition that went away once Brandon started dating Rebecca, but Gary was hoping it would come back now that everyone was back on good terms. Gary missed having his two favorite guys around, even with the added addition of Nick and Clyde.

"Y'all know y'all not right for putting me in the house with the kids," Gary said standing behind the bar in the garage. "I ain't got no damn kids."

"But you are a god dad so that's close enough." Brandon shrugged his shoulders.

"Man, that was supposed to be your position," Gary said filling up the shot glasses in front of him with Tequila. "Aye, Nasir is it too late for us to switch?"

"You know you're an asshole, right?" Nasir leaned over the table with the cue. "If it was up to Ashley neither of your asses would be the godparent, but Brandon was not the first choice and it had nothing to do with me and his beef."

"She hates me, but she loves my wife." Brandon shook his head. "Ain't that some shit?"

"You know how Ash gets," Nick said. "She can't stand you, but let me assure you that she loves you."

"Love...I doubt. Maybe slightly like." Brandon laughed.

"I thought the girls were bad, but you guys are one dysfunctional group of men," Clyde said, taking his turn at the pool table.

"Yet, you decided to date my sister." Nick tilted his head and laughed.

"Your sister is an angel. Truly perfect."

"An angel carrying a whole lot of baggage, but I'll let her be the one to tell you," Nick paused, "that's if she doesn't dump you first."

"Welp, I know who's going to object at our wedding," Clyde said, his fourth ball going into the hole.

"Don't get your hopes up. She's quick to call those off too."

All the guys looked at each and let out a laugh. A lot of drama unfolded at Ashley and Nasir's baby shower and Nicole calling off her engagement to cheating ass Derek was one of them. Nasir was too busy trying to get home to ice his face after Nick punched him to the floor. It wasn't until a day or two after his son was born that he found out Nicole ended her engagement.

"Am I missing something?" Clyde felt left out.

"Nick, leave that boy alone. He's clearly head over heels for your sister," Brandon said.

"Even I can see you're being a hater," Gary added.

"Hey, whose side are you guys on?" Nick folded his arms.

"The side of love," they said at the same time.

Nasir smiled, "Now, that's that twin shit I missed."

"Y'all come over here," Gary said filling his and Brandon's shot glasses. They had been taking back-to-back shots at the bar while Nasir and Clyde played pool and Nick threw darts around. "Let's make a toast to getting the brotherhood back together...and these two." Gary eyed Nick and Clyde.

"You really are an asshole," Nick said before taking his shot. "And damn proud of it."

* * *

Rebecca wasn't ready to tell the whole group she was pregnant. Out of everyone on the trip, only Monica, Ashley, and Nasir knew she was pregnant and she swore Ashley and Nasir to secrecy. She knew for a fact it was one thing they were good at. If Shantel hadn't been jealous of every woman in their circle and if Regina wasn't loyal to Ashley, she never would have found out Nasir cheated on her. Then when it came to Ashley's pregnancy, literally everyone hid it from Rebecca and Brandon. They tore into their asses about it, so they had no choice but to keep their mouths shut. Monica also agreed to keep Rebecca's pregnancy a secret until she was ready to spill the tea.

While the guys drank and played games, the women decided to keep it chill with a movie night and drinks. Rebecca volunteered to make the cocktails so she knew what was in her cup. While she made the girls lemon drops, she simply drank lemonade.

"So when are you going to tell everyone else?" Monica's eyes lit up, after realizing what Rebecca was doing.

"Not this weekend," She said looking towards the family room to make sure no one was within earshot. "Maybe when we get home, but for now let's not speak of any of this."

"Got it, but please don't take forever. I hate keeping things from Nikki and she's already mentioned you and Brandon working on having babies."

Rebecca put her finger over her lips; her way of telling Monica to relax. "I will tell her before I start to show, for now, help me take these drinks over to the ladies. I'll keep hold of mine."

Little Nasir and Ari were passed out in the fort she made in the middle of the floor and the rest of the ladies were sprawled out on the sofa with the movie waiting to play. Tonight's movie was **Sprung** starring Tisha Campbell and Paula Jai Parker. It was one of Rebecca's many favorites. One thing she enjoyed more than lounging around with her husband all day was watching a classic black film with a happily ever after.

"What do you think the guys are doing?" Nicole asked.

"Probably talking about us," Ashley responded.

"What else do they truly have to talk about?" Regina laughed. "We're practically their whole lives."

"Isn't that crazy how all of us are dating someone in this house?" Nikki took hold of Monica.

"Married. I'm married," Rebecca said flashing her ring.

"How could we forget with that massive rock on your finger." Kim giggled. "Do you ever take it off?"

"I try not to, but my husband says it gets in the way when I do that little thing that he likes," She winked.

"Don't be telling them, women, our business." Brandon came walking into the family room with the guys following behind, some clearly more wasted than the others. Brandon made his way over to the couch, picked up Rebecca, and placed her on his lap. "So you guys were just going to have a movie night without us?"

"That's kinda fucked up," Nasir said scooting next to Ashley. "Haven't I missed enough?"

"If you guys wanted to come to cuddle up with us that's all you had to say," Ashley responded.

"We want to be up under you b—"

"Gary," Regina said raising her hand.

"I was gonna say, beautiful women. Damn," Gary said putting his hand up before Regina slapped him.

"So, what are we watching?" Clyde plopped down next to Nicole and put his arms around her. He could see Nick rolling his eyes from the corner of his and Kim laughing at him.

"Sprung," Nicole answered.

"Let me guess who picked it?" Before he could answer everyone yelled out, "REBECCA."

32

Day 2

After watching **Sprung** and then **Woo**, the couples gathered their children and made their way back to the other house. Nick and Nasir were still pretty sober and wanted to sleep in a bed, not on the couch. Brandon and Gary on the other hand were wasted. Rebecca had to practically drag him into the bedroom and all plans of taking him down were canceled the minute he almost puked in her mouth.

In typical Rebecca fashion, she was up at 5:00 a.m. sharp, in the backyard with a yoga mat and her meditation playlist. The usual run she'd go on was out of the question since she was terrified of crossing paths with a snake or some other creature. Rebecca wasn't the only person awake that early in the morning. Nikki was sitting on a lounge chair typing away at her laptop like a mad woman. Rebecca hadn't noticed her until she was bent over in a downward-facing dog. The sight of Nikki almost sent her face first into the concrete. Luckily she was able to catch her balance until she managed to be in an upright position again.

Rolling up her mat, Rebecca made her way over to Nikki. "We

are supposed to be on a vacation, Why are you working?"

Continuing to stare at the screen, Nikki banged away at the letters on her keyboard. "I know I know," she glanced quickly at Rebecca, "it's just that I'm in the zone and I don't want to lose it. A few more paragraphs and I'll be satisfied."

Knowing the need to get something done when the creative juices are flowing through you, Rebecca didn't bother encouraging her to put the laptop away. It wasn't like anyone else was awake at the moment. They were dead to the world.

"Do you want me to bring you out some coffee, tea, anything?"

"Coffee please," Nikki answered softly. "I have a slight headache, but I couldn't sleep. I know it's going to catch up to me," she said, finally looking up to acknowledge Rebecca's presence.

"Coffee it is. I'll be back shortly."

"Thank you." Nikki smiled. "By the way, there's something different about you. Whatever it is..." she paused and examined Rebecca, "I like it."

"Something about officially becoming a Mrs. added an extra glow to me," she said placing her hands on her cheeks and grinning.

"Anything to show off that ring." Nikki laughed.

"I'm not sure which I love more," Rebecca said glaring into the stone, "the ring or him."

"Dick," Nikki slightly closed her laptop, "it's definitely dick."

"Yeah, that chocolate pop is pretty damn magical."

"Ew not a chocolate pop." Nikki laughed. "Let me get back to writing before you start going into detail about every vein and the way it curves or doesn't."

"It doesn't," Rebecca said skipping into the house.

* * *

"There you are, my handsome husband. Happy to see you're alive. I thought you weren't going to make it for brunch." Rebecca ran towards Brandon and jumped on him, wrapping her body around his.

"Someone has a whole lot of energy this morning."

"More like afternoon," she said before brushing her lips against his. "I didn't even get a taste of that morning wood."

"I see that baby in your belly hasn't suppressed your appetite for me," he whispered in her ear.

"It's only made me hornier." She licked his lips and walked back towards the kitchen.

"Wait," he quietly yelled, "come back here and show me."

"I guess I could go for another shower, but we have to hurry," she said turning back towards her husband and then off to the bedroom.

"If being married gets you that much ass I want to walk down the aisle *today*." Clyde grabbed Nicole by the waist. They had just entered the kitchen when they spotted the married couple running off like sneaky teenagers.

"That's the only reason you'd get married?" Nicole pushed him away from her slightly. "What about love?"

"Love is beautiful, but it's not everything."

"But pussy is?" She turned up her nose waiting on his answer. Nicole didn't want to get involved with a man whose only intention was fucking her. She was hoping and praying Clyde was different.

"Hey, now you're putting words in my mouth. Of course, love *and* sex are important, but I want to build a bond that no one can break. I want to be best friends with the woman I marry

162

first. I want to be able to trust her with my life and she trusts me with hers. I want to have something that will last always and forever," he said pulling Nicole into him. "Constant pussy is just a bonus," he said kissing her on the lips.

"You're cute but annoying." She giggled. "Let's go make our way down to the other house, so you can annoy my brother while you can."

"While I can. Are you gonna dump me like he said you would?"

"Did he say that to you? I'm going to kill him."

* * *

As one big family, they all enjoyed the brunch made for them by Ashley and Kim. Ashley brushed up on her cooking skills thanks to her 'retired' life. Most of her days were spent on the internet looking up new creations to make for her little family. On a few occasions, she and Nasir took cooking classes as a way to connect again. Kim agreed to help out. This was a way for her to show Ashley she was committed to building a genuine connection with her and to show her she wasn't going to let what happened with Nasir get in the way of that. Kim also knew how important it was to Nick. Nicole, who originally wasn't on team Kim, had a change of heart with time. At the beginning of Kim and Nick's relationship Nicole thought it was bullshit and assumed Kim was only around for a good time and a little extra help with her child. Just like Nick, Nicole is extremely protective when it comes to those she loves, but Kim made it clear she was in love with Nick and planned to stick beside him through whatever.

"Delicious," Monica moaned as she stuffed her mouth with

the cheesy shrimp and grits Ashley made.

"I ain't ever heard you moan like that for me," Nikki joked.

"You are mouth-watering baby," Monica winked at Nikki, "but this, this is fucking sensational."

"Sounds like you're going to need to put some of that between your thighs," Gary chuckled.

"There are children around. Control yourselves," Rebecca insisted.

"Sorry sis, but your bestie over there started it when she started making porno sounds." Gary laughed but immediately shut his mouth when Regina side-eyed him and then kicked him under the table.

Once everyone let their food digest they decided to take a dip in the pool. Ari made it clear that everyone would be on her "Mean Adults" list if they didn't go for a swim with her. Kim and Nick, brushed her off as they tended to do when she got overly excited. The moment she cleared her plate she put on her unicorn swimsuit, and pink life jacket, and got her pool toys. Rebecca was the first to volunteer to go in with her because it was clear she would go on her own if no one followed suit. Taking Rebecca's hand Ari screamed out, "Jump" and into the water, they went, hand-in-hand. When her head rose from under the water Brandon was standing at the edge of the pool looking at Rebecca with concern. Now that she was pregnant, he kept a close watch on her every move.

"We're okay," Rebecca assured him.

"Get in Uncle B." Ari splashed water at him and swam away.

"I'm going to get you." Brandon dived into the pool.

"Oh no! There's a shark behind you," Nasir yelled out. "I'll save you." He dived into the pool and wrestled around with Brandon.

"I'm safe now," she said waving her arms in the air. "Better get away from that shark before it eats you."

As she was talking, Brandon gained power over Nasir and dunked his head in the water.

"I told you." Ari giggled before jumping back into the pool.

"The biggest kids I know," Ashley said lowering herself into the pool next to Rebecca. "It's nice to see Nasir smile like this again. He really missed Brandon."

"I can tell. I never saw them be this playful when we dated," she said with hesitation.

"It's okay. you can say it. Most of us have dated someone here." Ashley looked over at Monica and Gary then started to laugh. Surprisingly they still had a friendly relationship despite the way he treated her in the past. He also hated that Brandon snatched her up for his project, so he gave her shit about it every chance he got. He had spent the majority of the morning trying to convince her to star in one of his films, but she wasn't having it. After filming for Brandon's show wrapped, she was looking to move on to other opportunities, especially if this first season didn't take off.

"Back in high school that's all those two did. Gary on the other hand spent all his time trying to impress the girls. Most of them wanted Brandon because he was nicer and wasn't a showoff, yet they all ended up with their heads between Gary's legs." Ashley shook her head.

"Hey, I guess they said he was close enough to the real thing." Rebecca laughed.

"Basically. I know we haven't got to talk about it much, but how are you feeling?" Ashley asked, her eyes lowering to Rebecca's belly. "You should start showing in a few months."

Checking her surroundings before responding, she leaned in,

"I feel like myself, I'm not sick or anything yet, just tired, but that's getting better. Watching Brandon with Ari and your son has me thrilled. I know he's going to be an amazing father. I wouldn't want to go through this experience with anyone else."

"Yeah, as much as he thinks I hate him, he's a great guy. I would have taken him as Little Nasir's god dad over Gary," she said looking over at Brandon, who was now gliding Little Nasir across the water. The children were putting him to work.

"Trust me, without the title he is still going to do for that boy like he helped bring him into the world himself."

"I do not doubt it." Ashley smiled and hugged Rebecca before making her way over to her son. "I got him, go spend some time with your wife. We'll see you guys at the house for the BBQ later."

* * *

Stripping out of her wet swimsuit, Rebecca walked into the shower and let the water from the shower head cover her from head to toe. There was one located on the wall and then another on the ceiling of the shower. Coming up behind his wife, Brandon put a mix of shampoo and conditioner in the palms of his hand and massaged it through her curly hair, giving extra attention to her scalp.

"You're so good to me," she said as he washed the shampoo out of her hair and she cleaned her body.

"If I weren't you wouldn't have married me." He turned her towards him, pulling her in for a kiss. The water pounded against her breast causing her nipples to protrude. Unable to control his desire, Brandon took her breast into the palm of his hands; caressing them while gently pulling at her nipple, sending a moan through her. The sound of her moaning made his dick jump. Rebecca took him into her hand and stroked his dick.

"Fuck," he groaned as she sped up her stroke.

"I want you inside of me."

Using her neck as his canvas, Brandon covered it in kisses while teasing her clit with his fingers. "How much?" He asked, gliding his fingers across her pussy, making her body shiver. Brandon wanted his wife to teeter on the edge of ecstasy before dipping into her honey.

Grinding against his fingers she moaned, "More than anything in this world." She sped the movement of her hips and continued, "I wish I could take this dick with me everywhere I go."

"I guess I should go get my dick molded into a dildo for you," he said turning his wife around and bending her forward. Rebecca placed her hands on the shower wall as he teased her opening with the tip of his dick. "But it won't feel nothing like the real thing," he continued.

"I'll be the judge of that," she said pushing herself onto his dick while massaging her clit.

Taking hold of her breast, Brandon slides deep into her honey, pulling out slowly. Using her muscles, Rebecca wrapped her pussy around his dick, as if she were saying *don't go*. Brandon pounded back into her, grunting in pleasure as she did Kegels on his dick. "You-you're gonna make me cum."

"Cum for me Daddy," Rebecca moaned as she bounced against him violently. "Fill me up."

Wrapping his hand around her neck, Brandon matched his wife's movements. Getting weak in the knees, he released himself inside of her as she screamed out his name. Pulling her up, he held her from behind waiting for their bodies to settle down from the orgasm they shared.

"The real thing will always be my favorite," Rebecca whimpered, still trying to catch her breath.

"Round two?"

"Husband, let's get you washed up first."

"I'm just going to sweat again," he said inserting his fingers into Rebecca. "Feels like you're ready for another go anyway."

33

Day 3

The trip turned out better than anyone expected. It was the first time the entire group had come together in years without any drama. Last night everyone came back to the house to enjoy the dinner Rebecca and Brandon whipped up for them: BBQ ribs, links, lamb, mashed potatoes, mac-n-cheese, and creamed spinach to name a few. They drank and played dominoes, and black card revoked. The night ended with karaoke and a dip in the Jacuzzi. Rebecca only put her feet in because she was advised by her doctor not to take super hot baths, so a Jacuzzi was definitely out of the question. Something about the body overheating being dangerous for the baby. Whatever the reason she wasn't taking any chances with this pregnancy.

To Nick's disliking, Clyde had officially asked Nicole to be his girlfriend, but they agreed to take things slow. Rebecca slightly laughed when he asked her because he had a stupid grin on his face and she knew it meant one thing—Nicole had finally let him get a taste of what was between her legs. Clyde was the type to have sex with a girl and get sprung immediately after.

There was no doubt in Rebecca's mind that was the reason he put a title on their relationship. He didn't want anyone else coming around snatching her up.

"You haven't even known her long," Nick whined, before being shut up by Kim. Apparently, they hadn't been dating long either before he professed his dying love for her and took on the role of stepdaddy.

Regina ended the trip with a surprise therapy session with Dr. Bell. Regina knew most of them would have objected if she brought up the idea in advance. For them to truly come together and be the 'family' they swore they were, everything needed to be put out on the table. Healing needed to start from all sides. The trip initially started as a plan to get Nasir and Brandon back on track, but everyone had shit they needed to mend.

Rebecca prayed to the heavens when she realized what was going on. Everyone had been getting along so well and she didn't want them to end up back at square one; angry, hurt, and resentful. Fortunately for her, everything turned out well. Nasir admitted that his desire to be the perfect partner and businessman, along with the trauma of Ashley's past had played a major part in his past drinking problems and anger.

Nasir had never grown up in an abusive environment. He went to school, and church, played sports, and spent all his time with the twins. For the better part of his life, he was sheltered and that was rare for a boy growing up in Richmond, CA. When Ashley and her siblings came into his life a lot of the trauma they went through caused him to have some sort of PTSD. It made him feel like he was inadequate and unable to protect the people he loved.

"I didn't know that was possible," Ashley said.

"There are many reasons one may become mentally and

physically abusive towards others and themselves." Before continuing to speak to the group Dr. Bell looked at Nasir and asked him if she had permission to disclose some of what they talked about in their private sessions. Once Nasir gave her the go-ahead she continued to speak. "For example, Nasir spent about five years with Ashley. From the start of their relationship, he had to witness and or hear her and her siblings being abused countless times. Nasir and his family were a safe place for Ashley, but he knew it was only temporary. Ashley had to return home to the toxicity. During that, no one ever asked Nasir how what was being done in Ashley's home affected him."

"Go on," Ashley said looking at Dr. Bell, who had paused to give her and her siblings the box of tissues.

"Nasir was put in a spot where he wanted to protect you and be strong, but you guys were only children. Nasir was in a situation that he had no control over. When a person feels like they've lost control of everything or are no longer needed, they tend to lose control of themselves. Nasir hadn't acknowledged these feelings until the two of you went on your paths."

"That's some deep shit," Gary said.

"Unfortunately, it took him hurting someone else to realize he was dealing with something internally. Instead of getting help, he chooses to bury his feeling and sins deep inside as if they never took place," Dr. Bell clasped her hands together, "but the thing about that is, not everything can remain buried. What is done in the dark *always* comes to light."

From that point on the therapy session had gotten deeper than anyone could have imagined. Kim revealed to the group that for years she remained scared and unwilling to open up to anyone. That the mental damage was worst than the physical.

She explained that because of one night in college, she had ruined a relationship between Ari and her father.

"You have nothing to do with that man not wanting to be a father to his child," Dr. Bell assured her.

They ended up setting up an appointment to meet when her calendar opened. Kim had stopped seeing her therapist shortly after meeting Nick, but she held onto a lot of what she learned in those sessions. Now that Nasir would be a constant in her life she figured it might be a good idea to start again just in case she was triggered. *It's also nice to speak to a person you don't personally know*, she thought.

During that session, Clyde learned more about Nicole than he had learned in their month of dating one another. He now had an understanding of why Nick was giving him a hard time. The two of them had gone through shit no child should have to.

By the end of their group session, everyone's shit was on front street, including Gary's experience with an older woman when he was only twelve. Monica's past with abusive men and a man who left her for a wife she didn't even know he had in the beginning. Nikki's commitment issues and insecurities. In middle school, Nikki's eating disorder started and lasted up until a year ago. She told no one, not even Monica. It was one of the reasons she was scared to move in with Monica, but she blamed it all on her lack of trust in their relationship.

They were a damaged group, but they agreed that they had each other to lean on and there was no turning back. Forever and always they would be tethered to one another, whether they liked it or not.

* * *

"So besides the obvious... you losing your parents," Monica said staring Brandon down, "are you truly the only one of us that's not extremely fucked up? Like this man is truly perfect."

"And what am I?" Gary turned his nose up at Monica.

"Like the rest of us." Nikki smiled and patted him on the back as she walked by.

"Y'all might look alike, but there can only be one perfect twin." Monica giggled.

"Yet, I'm the one you liked," he said arrogantly.

"You were just easy," Regina said. "I could have taken you down the night I met you, but I needed you to get your shots and some home training first."

"Woof Woof!" Monica gave Regina a high-five, both laughing until they felt cramps on their sides.

"Very funny," Gary said smacking Regina on the ass.

"Aye, don't be ganging up on my brother. I am not perfect but I did spend a lot of time making sure everyone around me stayed out of bullshit. I didn't have time for life to truly fuck me up," Brandon said.

"And that right there is your flaw," Rebecca said. "You don't put yourself first."

"Okay Dr. Young," Ashley yelled from the kitchen. She was eavesdropping on the discussion while making a drink for the road. Nasir was back at the other house with Nick getting everything packed up.

"And to think I thought I was flawless in your eyes." He pulled Rebecca in, gazing deep into her eyes, "Am I not?"

"Do you want me to lie?" She whispered seductively in his ear.

"If it's gonna sound that damn sexy."

"Husband, you are perfect," she said licking his lips, "to me."

173

"Ugh, get a room already," Monica rolled her eyes. "I'm going to go finish packing up my bag."

Once everyone was packed up they locked up the house and met out front; giving each other hugs and kisses as if they wouldn't be seeing each other again.

"Thank you, guys, for all coming. I needed this," Ashley said, "seriously."

"Aww babe, was I stressing you out," Nasir said kissing her forehead.

"Nigga," Gary titled his head, "you were stressing every last one of us."

The group laughed in agreement.

"No, but for real. Me and Ashley are happy we were able to make this happen, especially with everyone's schedule."

"We'll have to do it again and soon," Regina added.

"Yeah, because in about 6 7 months I'm going to be laying in somebodies hospital bed."

Brandon looked at his wife in shock as if this was the first time he was hearing her say she was pregnant. "I thought you wanted to wait," he said into her ear.

"It just seemed like the right time."

Everyone else examined her, trying to find a bump, but it wasn't there.

"I knew there was something different about you." Nikki lit up.

"What's in 7 months?" Gary asked.

"Gary, are you slow? Monica asked

"Do you seriously have to ask?" Regina laughed. "Babe, you're going to be an uncle."

"You're pregnant?" He asked Rebecca, ignoring what the women were obviously telling him.

"Yes Gary, I'm pregnant," she confirmed.

Running over to her, Gary picked up his sister-in-law and started spinning around. Gary had never shown Rebecca this much affection. He was smiling from ear to ear.

Brandon pulled at his arm. "Yo, put my wife down before somebody thinks you're the daddy."

"I'm going to be an uncle, that's close enough."

"Yo, you're sick as fuck," Nasir blurted out.

"I'm happy you're happy, but when I ask you to babysit or change a diaper I bet not hear not one complaint." Rebecca chuckled as he put her down and finally embraced his brother.

"So when do we start planning the baby shower?" Gary asked.

"If you aren't this fucking ecstatic when I get pregnant I'm legit going to murder you." Regina had he hands on her hips mugging Gary.

"You'd have to move in with me first," he said sticking his tongue out at her.

"Asshole," she screamed out causing everyone to laugh. They'd been calling him one the whole weekend.

"Back to what I was saying," he turned back to Rebecca and Brandon, "baby shower?

"Hold your horses," Brandon said putting up his hand.

"Yeah, I need to tell my mom first, but maybe we can have it in Seattle. My mom would love the company."

"Sounds like we've got our next trip planned," Brandon pulled in Rebecca, "now, can we get out of here before I burn to death? It's fucking hot."

34

Gender Reveal

Twins, Rebecca and Brandon were having twins. Rebecca knew it was a possibility but it completely went over her head since it's a rare occurrence, even in cases of the mother or father being a twin themselves. Though everyone knew she was having a baby she had yet to tell anyone it was going to be two of them, so they'd be getting a double reveal today.

"Ready for today my beautiful wife?"

"Ready for it to begin and then quickly end," Rebecca admitted. "I'm tired and I still need to have a discussion with Diane about how we are going to handle the publication while I'm on leave."

Brandon sat behind Rebecca and massaged her back. "You can worry about that another day. It's not like you're going on leave for at least another two or three months. Today I want you to have fun and relax. It's all about you."

"Us," Rebecca corrected him, "and those months are going to fly by."

"Everything will work out the way it needs to. Please don't

stress about it," he said wrapping his hands around her stomach and rubbing it. "What time does your mom get in?"

"Monica should actually be on her way to get her from LAX. They should be here around noon and we should be starting promptly at 2:00 p.m."

"Good luck." Brandon laughed. "You're friends are rarely on time."

"My friends are *your* friends. Now hush and come rub my feet."

"I wish I could come rub on something else," Brandon smirked.

"Uh uh not happening. I am not in the mood, not today."

"Yeah, I know. I'll just have to take another cold shower."

"This is what happens when you knock your wife up with twins," Rebecca said caressing her bump.

"And I'll be putting some more up in you when these bad boys drop."

"If you never want to have sex again...go for it." She grinned.

* * *

The Young household was decorated beautifully; the all-white family room and the backyard was covered in equal parts blue and pink, matching the parents perfectly. Rebecca wore an ombré pink and blue backless v-neck spaghetti strapped dress, which flowed to the floor and had a split on each side. Brandon wore powder blue slacks and a short sleeve white button up, with custom pink buttons.

"I have the prettiest wife on the planet," Brandon said, admiring the beauty standing before him.

"I don't feel like it," she whined.

"Mama Athena," Brandon yelled out, "get in here and tell your daughter how beautiful she is."

"Can't we just tell everyone to go home? Monica can send everyone a text telling them the great news." Monica was the only person who knew the gender of the twins. Rebecca informed the doctor they would be doing a gender reveal, so she wrote the gender down and sealed it in an envelope. Rebecca knew it was either going to be a boy or a girl because Monica wouldn't have been able to compose herself if she knew twins were growing inside her best friend.

"NO, we cannot." Athena came walking into the master bedroom. "I did not spend three hours on a plan for you to say you want to cancel. I don't know what made you want to do a gender reveal anyway. Back in my day a few people would come over, drink, eat, open gifts, and go on their merry way."

"I thought it would be cute," Rebecca admitted, "but now I just feel overwhelmed. The sound of all those damn people in my house is only making me anxious."

"If it were up to me I'd tell everyone to go home," Brandon assured his wife, "but your mom is right, she and a few other people had to travel quite a ways."

Rebecca put her hands on her hips and said, "Well, they can stay and everyone else can go."

"Son, go entertain your guest while I speak with Momzilla over here."

Brandon hugged Athena and kissed his wife before walking out of the room and closing the door behind him. Monica had already begun entertaining guests and it sounded like a round of karaoke was going on. He could hear Nasir and Gary butchering one of his and Rebecca's favorite songs, "Differences" by Ginuwine.

Athena walked over to the velvet couch sitting in the corner of their room. "Come sit next to mommy," she said patting her hand on the spot next to her. "Tell me what's really going on because I know it's not just the hormones. You look gorgeous by the way, glow and all."

"Thank you, mommy."

"You haven't called me mommy since that disastrous first wedding of yours. What did Brandon do?"

Rebecca giggled, finally letting a smile peak through her blank expression. "My husband is absolutely perfect. No complaints when it comes to that beautiful man. I'm just nervous and overwhelmed with this whole idea of motherhood."

"Coming from your mother, you have nothing to worry about. You have a supportive group of friends, me, and a husband who's going to be there every step of the way. Besides, you're six months pregnant, and ain't no putting that baby back in the sack."

Rebecca laughed. "That's nasty mom."

Athena touched her daughter's stomach. "Being nasty is what got you all knocked up and emotional."

"Can I tell you something?"

"Anything," Athena said with a look of worry.

"It was supposed to be a surprise, but we're having twins. How am I supposed to manage a home, career, and motherhood all at the same time?"

"You are blessed baby girl. You went from believing you couldn't carry a child at all to two blessings. There is no playbook on how to be a perfect mother. You just have to have faith in the man upstairs, yourself, and your husband. Know that raising those babies isn't all on you. If Brandon is the man I believe him to be you will never feel alone in this journey."

Rebecca's eyes swelled with tears. "You have no idea how relieved I am to have you here, still living and breathing, giving me strength and courage. I pray I'm as great of a mom as you've been to me." Rebecca rested her head on her mother's shoulders.

"You'll be better. Let's go wipe those tears and reapply that liner."

After almost three hours locked in her room, Rebecca finally came down to take pictures with her family and friends. She was able to play one game, which was all she had the energy for. Brandon announced that Rebecca was feeling under the weather, but she sent a message for everyone to enjoy themselves. Once she came down, most people stood clear, not wanting to be a bother to the mother...or get whatever she might be contagious with. Rebecca thanked him with kisses for finding a way to cover up for her.

"Alright, everyone... it's time," Monica announced. "Make your way out to the backyard."

Sitting outside was a movie projector and screen surrounded by a blue, pink, and white balloon wreath. Two custom rocking chairs embedded with their last name, Young, sat in the middle of the lawn. Taking Rebecca by the hand, Brandon led her to her seat.

"I wonder what this is?" she said sitting down slowly.

"Whatever it is, I'm sure we'll love it," Brandon said taking her hand into his.

Now that everyone was seated, Gary pressed play. The first thing that popped on the screen was compiled videos of Rebecca and Brandon's late parents and their parenting journey; the sonograms, the doctor's visits, the day Brandon and Rebecca were born, the first steps, and birthdays. Rebecca squeezed

Brandon's hand tighter, hoping it would help her fight back tears. After the video and photo collage went off, videos of their relatives and friends taking guesses at the gender popped up. A few even added their thoughts about her having twins.

Clyde was one of those people. "Not to be a jerk or anything, but my bestie is looking a little on the heavy side for there to only be one baby baking. I bet it's two boys, you know since Brandon is a twin," he said.

"So you're calling me fat behind my back?" Rebecca turned around looking to see where Clyde was sitting.

"Technically I said it to your face," he said pointing at the screen.

"Such a gentleman," Brandon said sarcastically and focused his attention back on the video.

The last slide was a video of Monica pretending to be a pregnant Rebecca and Gary playing Brandon. Monica was laid out on the exam table with her shirt lifted as the doctor moved the transducer across Monica's fake silicone belly.

"You guys really went all out for this," Rebecca said laughing.

"How the hell did you guys find time to film in a real doctor's office?" Brandon chuckled.

"It's us," Gary smirked, "we have connections."

"Yeah, mine," she said when she heard a familiar voice. It was her doctor's, then she heard the sound of a baby's heartbeat. It was a video Rebecca had sent to Monica after getting an ultrasound.

In unison, Monica and Gary asked, "What are we having?" then a voice on the screen said, "Mom and dad, turn around." When Rebecca and Brandon stood up to face their loved ones all they saw were pink balloons floating into the sky and pink confetti flying everywhere. There were two photographers; one behind them and another behind their family. Gary also had a drone flying around to catch every angle and expression.

"We're having girls." Rebecca smiled and kissed Brandon like it was their wedding day all over again.

"And to think you didn't want to come down for this moment." He broke away from their kiss.

"Did I hear her say, girls?" They heard someone say.

"Like girls with an s as in two," another person said.

"Should we tell them now?" Brandon whispered.

"Let's go for it."

"Attention attention," Brandon called out, "my wife would like to tell you all something."

All ears and eyes were on Rebecca.

"For those on the video taking guesses, my husband and I are indeed having twins," she said shaking her hips and rubbing her belly.

"I knew it," Clyde shouted. "Run me my money, Gary."

"Really, y'all was taking bets on my wife's womb? That's your friend." Brandon shook his head and laughed.

"And that's your brother...by blood. You're stuck."

35

Seattle w/ The Crew

"Everyone is staring at me."

"Fuck everyone, you look fucking gorgeous and we refuse to make you spend your New Year's Eve in the house." Nikki rubbed Rebecca's stomach. "It's not like you at a fucking club taking shots."

Rebecca decided she wanted to have her baby shower on New Year's day, so she hit up the crew and let them know to take off. Clyde, Nicole, Nick, and Kim couldn't make it so a few weeks before they left for Seattle, they had a small surprise baby shower for her at Nasir's place. He was working hard to stay on good terms with everyone.

Rebecca wanted to spend New Year's Eve at her mom's but the ladies refused to let her spend the night inside so they dragged her to a last-minute jazz concert downtown. Once it was over they would be able to make it home in time to shower and get comfortable before the countdown. They would also be able to see the fireworks from Athena's backyard.

"Seriously, forget those people," Ashley added.

"Yeah, *fuck* anybody who has an issue with a pregnant woman wanting to listen to some live jazz with her family on New Year's Eve," Monica said loud enough for the whole room to hear.

Everyone laughed when they noticed their eyes were no longer on them.

"Monica," Athena shook her head, "language."

"I'm sorry Mrs. Bloom, but I will not stand for the disrespect and mistreatment of pregnant women," Monica shouted out dramatically.

"We should have taken her ass to an improv show or something." Gary chuckled.

"Life is my improv class asshole."

"If you guys say one more curse word my mom is going to kick all our asses."

"Starting with this one here," Athena said smacking Monica's thigh. "Who told you to come outside in that little ass dress. It's freezing." Monica had on a shimmering gold mini-dress with a plunging neckline. If it went down any further she'd be naked.

"Language Athena," Gary mimicked.

"Brandon, get your brother before there's one less twin in this world," Athena warned.

"Mom," Rebecca giggled, "I don't think I'm in any condition to bail you out if you murder someone."

Rebecca was due the first week of February, but she felt like she could give birth at any moment. She and Brandon planned a home birth, but she wanted it to be in her home.

"Guys, let's go get the ladies some drinks," Brandon said, not doubting his mother-in-law would follow through with her threat.

"Whew, I ain't know Rebecca's mama was that tough," Nasir said once they got to the bar. "Good thing you married her and not me," he said patting Brandon on the shoulder.

"She loves me. We have no issues. I know how to behave," he said looking at Gary.

"I shouldn't have to behave. I didn't marry her daughter."

"Just when I think you've grown that little asshole on your shoulder comes to say hi," Brandon laughed, "but at least you try."

* * *

Rebecca's mom lived 15 minutes from Downtown Seattle in a beautiful 6 bed 4 bath home that sat up against the lake— perfect for any occasion. Athena was overjoyed when Rebecca told her she wanted to have her baby shower there. Rebecca never understood why her parents bought such a luxurious home when it was only the two of them in it, but it was perfect for a couple who wanted to retire in peace, yet still, be surrounded by community.

Walking into the kitchen, Rebecca watched as her mom danced around to "That's The Way Love Goes" by Janet Jackson and sipped on a mimosa, while she scrambled eggs.

"Is this a part of your morning routine?"

Athena looked over her shoulder. "Only when I'm celebrating my baby having a baby. Any other day it's coffee." She smirked.

"Glad to see cooking and dancing is still a part of your mornings."

Every Saturday morning, Athena would wake up bright and early. The music would blast through the house, her way of waking Rebecca and her dad. She'd always been a morning person, so she would be dressed by the time breakfast was on the table. Whenever Rebecca saw her dancing with her cup of coffee, which was spiked with Kahlua, it was bound to be a good day. The mimosa in her flute let Rebecca know today was going to be memorable.

"Go turn that music up a little louder. Almost time to eat," she said swaying her hips.

"Brushing up on those hip rolls I see." Rebecca laughed as she walked towards the speaker system.

"I'm trying to stay as young as I can for as long as I can."

"Smells good in here Mrs. Bloom," Nasir said walking through the door.

"Morning run?" Rebecca asked.

"You know it."

"Thank you, sweetie," Athena said. "I didn't even see you get up."

"He wakes up at like 5 in the morning. You definitely weren't going to see him," Rebecca answered for him.

"Yeah, you had my wife stuck on that outrageous schedule. I'm so happy these babies have allowed me to get some rest," Brandon said walking into the kitchen. He reached out to take a piece of bacon, but Athena slapped his hand away. "Wait for everyone to wake up so we can eat as a family."

"Sorry mom," Brandon said sitting down at the table.

Nasir shook his head and laughed. Rebecca's mom was a piece of work and played no games. She sort of reminded him of the twin's mom. "Do I have time to take a quick shower? Would hate for you all to smell my funk."

"Go for it, sweetie."

"How come you don't call me sweetie?" Brandon asked.

"Because you got the girl and he didn't."

"Heyyyy," Nasir yelled out, "I heard that."

"Mom, what am I going to do with you?" Rebecca shook her

head, while Brandon laughed.

"Love me," she answered.

* * *

Nikki and Regina were in charge of setting up decorations for the shower, Ashley was on kitchen duty, and Monica would be on hosting duty; getting the games started and keeping a track record of guest and their gifts, so the parents could send thank you cards when time permitted.

"I know Rebecca wanted to have everything set up outside but I went out there and it's freezing. I don't think the guest will enjoy sitting in the cold for hours," Regina informed Athena.

"You're absolutely right. It's beautiful out there, but it's not worth anyone getting sick, especially the mom. We need her to stay strong for those babies."

"And we do not want a repeat of the gender reveal," Nikki added.

"Oh, don't even remind me. Almost missed the whole shindig," Athena laughed, "but hormones will do that to you."

"Good thing this is the last event she has to worry about before pushing those girls out. I cannot wait to see their faces." Nikki smiled.

"I'll be booking my flight immediately when the time comes so make sure you ladies are around."

"Miss Athena, just put us on speed dial and me and Monica will come running," Nikki replied.

"You ladies are going to have to show me how to do that before you leave. I may look and move like I'm young, but that technology stuff is not my thing."

Around 1:00 p.m. Athena's friends began arriving at her

house. Rebecca and Athena didn't have much family left, but her mother created her own little family within her community who were happy to see her become a grandmother. Like Rebecca, she had accepted that it may not ever happen, at least not in her lifetime, so when she got the news she cried for hours and then proceeded to tell all her book club friends and a few of her neighbors. Rebecca hardly knew any of these people, but she knew letting her mother throw her a baby shower was one of her dreams. A few extra things for the baby wouldn't hurt either. They planned to have everything shipped to their home, but she was hoping her mom shared her registry and the shipping option that was given to them.

While the ladies stayed in eating, playing guessing games, and coming up with baby names, the guys hit a cigar bar downtown. Athena told them this was a ladies-only event and to get lost. There were no objections. Nasir and the twins put on their best fits and cologne then headed out to enjoy the town like old times. This time around, Nasir would be steering clear of all women. Whenever he went out with the twins, he seemed to run into a woman from his past and it always landed him in some shit. He would not allow that to happen anymore. Ashley was his only always and forever. He made up his mind and nothing or anyone was going to change that. Nasir enjoyed the home and family he created.

"Ready to officially be a daddy?" Nasir asked Brandon.

"It's all I've ever wanted. To be honest I was terrified it wouldn't happen for us. She tried to pull away from me for that exact reason, but to keep her I was willing to miss out on that part of life."

"God doesn't give us what we want until he knows we are ready. You and Rebecca were ready and you guys took the correct steps. Dated, made it official, moved in together and you know the rest. It was divine timing."

"My prayer we're for sure answered," Brandon said puffing gently on his cigar.

"Why must you niggas always be so deep," Gary said leaning back into the brown leather chair. "Can't we talk about bitches or something?"

"Niiiggggaa," Brandon laughed, "you are practically married. You don't got no bitches to talk about and if you did Regina would leave your ass at the drop of a dime."

"Yeah, you right," Gary said looking around the cigar bar.

"Relax, she's not here." Nasir chuckled.

Laughing Brandon said, "Remember that used to be you... looking around to see if my *wife* was coming for you whenever we were out somewhere."

"You gonna emphasize that wife word every time ain't you?" Nasir said, glaring down at the table.

"I gotta remind you just in case Ashley hits you on some 'maybe we should go back to being friends' shit and you try to come through and steal my *wife*," Brandon emphasized again.

"Ha ha ha very funny," Nasir said sarcastically. "Don't nobody want your *wife* when I have one of my own?"

"Huh?" Gary propped up in his seat. "You niggas sure know how to keep secrets."

"When did this happen?" Brandon asked.

"You know when me and Ashley took Little Nasir to San Diego?"

"Yea, right before we had the gender reveal."

"Well, we went out there to elope."

"Nigga what? You telling me Ashley finally locked you down and you ain't put up a fight?" Brandon asked.

189

"It was my idea. She was hesitant and I practically had to beg and plead before she agreed, but I know she was it for me. I don't want to look no further and the thought of losing her for good didn't feel right to me."

"When Rebecca hears about this she's going to try to plan a whole damn wedding. Brandon laughed.

"Wow, so I'm the only one without a ring on my finger. I know I'm a better nigga than you two."

"Bro, you make it sound like Regina the one that's supposed to be proposing to you," Brandon said.

"Shit, she might as well. Seems like she's calling all the shots in the relationship. I might as well let her do everything on her terms while I sit back and relax."

"Sound a little upset there," Nasir joked.

To Brandon and Nasir's surprise, he admitted he was. Gary was ready to move forward with Regina, but she was still giving him pushback. He stopped bringing up the move and he had been going to couples therapy with her faithfully for months. There was nothing else he could do but wait.

"I hate that I'm not getting what I want when I want, but she's worth the wait."

* * *

Walking back into Athena's place, the guys found the ladies cleaning up and Rebecca sound asleep in the massage chair.

"Long day?" Brandon asked.

"I think my friends put her to sleep with all their book talk."

"It was a bit much," Nikki laughed, "but they were adorable."

"We'll be reading one of your books next." Athena winked.

"TMI," Brandon said covering his ears.

"You act like you haven't read my books."

"That doesn't mean I want to hear my mother-in-law talk about them." He scrunched up his nose.

Ashley was in the kitchen washing dishes when Gary came snooping around trying to see if he could see a ring on her finger.

"What the fuck are you doing?" Ashley yelled when he snatched her hand from out the sink almost causing her to break a glass.

"You not gonna tell her don't be cussing Miss Athena?" Gary slurred his words.

"Here he goes embarrassing me," Regina said shaking her head. "Don't mind him."

"Sorry mom, he got a little emotional early and ended up taking too many shots," Brandon said trying to clean up Gary's mess. Brandon had never seen Gary be so in love that it caused him to act like an ass. He was always so sure about himself when it came to women.

"What's got him so emotional?" Athena asked out of curiosity.

"This," Gary said taking Ashley's left hand and raising it in the air.

"How much did he drink?" Regina said speed walking towards him.

Laughter filled the room as Gary looked at Ashley's empty ring finger, counting each finger out loud. All the noise woke up Rebecca, but no one noticed her short struggle to lift out of the chair. Holding her back she walked over to the kitchen where everyone was standing.

"Why is everyone being so dang loud?"

"Gary is over her acting like a crackhead again." Monica

laughed at herself.

Realizing what Gary was doing, Ashley slipped her hand from his grip and said, "If I'm not mistaken I think he just realized he's the only man in the group left without a wife and now he's having a mental breakdown."

"You guys are not making this easy for me," Regina said looking around the room.

"Sorry," Ashley mouthed, knowing what Regina was going through.

"Congrats."

"Congratulations guys."

"When?" Rebecca asked.

"Right before your reveal," she answered.

"I'm so happy for you," Rebecca walked over to hug Ashley. "When are we celebrating?"

"We wanted to wait until you two got settled with the babies," Ashley answered.

"Why am I always the last to do everything?" Gary cried out.

Putting her hand on her forehead in embarrassment, Regina took Gary by the hand. "If you all would excuse me, I'm going to take my manchild to bed."

"Bless your heart," Athena said embracing Regina. "You're a good woman."

"Is he going to be alright?" Rebecca asked.

"Let's hope so," Brandon said laughing.

"I love this friend group." Nikki giggled. "It's the kind of dysfunction I've been missing. Let's stay this way."

"Always," Ashley said.

"And forever," Rebecca concluded.

About the Author

Sydney Reneé is a Bay Area native and mother of one. She discovered her love for writing around the age of 17 when she created her first blog with dreams of starting a magazine. Her passion quickly turned toward creating relatable characters and experiences within her blog post, poems, and fictional stories

Sydney Reneé's stories are centered around strong black women and the ups and downs they face in daily life; love, heartbreak, friendships, insecurities, and more. With each book she hopes she can continue to be an inspiration to all women going through what we call life, reminding them that it's never too late to go after your dreams and speak your truth.

In her spare time, she enjoys spending time with family, reading, watching k-dramas, concerts, and going to Napa for wine and good fun.

You can connect with me on:

- https://linktr.ee/thediaryofshe
- https://twitter.com/TheDiaryofShe1
- https://www.facebook.com/thediaryofshe

Also by Sydney Reneé

In Love With An Oakland Hot Boy
London Robertson had always been treated like a queen on a throne by her father Marcus, who was one of the biggest pimps in Oakland, California. Besides the occasional bullshit she had to put up with due to her mother's lifestyle choice, life, for her, was great.She lived in a huge mansion, was going to be 18 soon, and had everything she had ever wanted until the relationship with her father took a turn for the worse...sending her running into the arms of the one person he couldn't stand most—her best friend's brother Eric.

Thinking she's finally found her fairytale ending, she gives herself to Eric only be treated like a prisoner in her own home with no one to turn to when the shit hits the fan. The man who saved her life is turning out to be a man she doesn't even recognize anymore.

Will London be able to repair the relationship with her father and get away from Eric before things turn deadly, or will she find herself living the same life that she vowed to always stay away from?